Don't the Moon
Look Lonesome

Don't the Moon Look Lonesome

DON ASHER

New York 1967 *Atheneum*

In Memory of My Father

Don't the moon look lone-some,
  shinin' through the trees?
Don't your house look lone-some,
  when your baby packs up to leave?

RUSHING / BASIE / DURHAM

Don't the Moon
Look Lonesome

One

On the morning of his fourth day in San Francisco, Jules Roman received this communiqué from the Superintendent of Schools of Willimouth, Connecticut:

For my records, in accordance with the terms of your six months' leave of absence commencing September 1, 1966, would you kindly remit an official transcript of your present course of study at San Francisco State College.

I wish you a pleasant and constructive six months.

Yours sincerely,
H. B. Ellis

"Jesus, I thought I had more time."

Six months to be exact.

He went to the refrigerator, dug into a pint of marble fudge ice cream and read the letter again. He had had little intention of actually enrolling at State (considering his formal education closed as of 1964) and only slightly more of returning to the Willimouth school system where for two grinding years his fifth-grade students had been stomping his bones unmercifully. But he figured he had six months' grace in which to review the matter, get the feel of sunny Cal and leisurely examine the prospects for a new life out here. Still, with nothing immediate in the offing, with no alternate avocation going for him, it would be difficult to sever the lifeline feeding in a steady $5,600 for thirty-eight weeks' work with $400 annual increments.

Spooning out more of the marble fudge, he began drafting a reply to Superintendent Ellis:

. . . taken the liberty of altering my plans to enroll at S. F. State . . . stimulating environment leads me to believe that I can utilize my time better, best . . . *most constructively* by informally immersing myself, embarking on . . . *steeping* myself in the cultural and historical atmosphere, lore . . . *traditions* of this legendary city . . .

H. B. Ellis' astringent reply crossed the continent in no time at all:

DEAR MR. ROMAN,

I am shocked and appalled that you should without sanction have taken it upon yourself to abrogate the terms of your leave. For your personal satisfaction and in the best interests of the Willimouth School Department I respectfully suggest that you submit to me, without delay, an official letter of resignation.

Yours very truly,
H. B. ELLIS

Crazy. Done and done. Expedited. The lifeline severed swiftly, virtually painlessly. With a burst of elation and optimism he felt he would be eternally grateful to H.B.

He immediately complied with the superintendent's request, then wrote to his brother relating the news and asking him to send on additional personal belongings. And Art, buddy, break it gently to the old guy.

Two

Struck squarely in the eyes the following morning by a shaft of northern California sunlight, he came awake and for an alarming moment or two had no idea where he was. Then something in the sunbeam's texture, an unfamiliar iridescence, jogged his senses and, remembering, he felt at once giddy and apprehensive. Head under the pillow, shielding his vision against this marvelous light, he focused inwardly on images not yet a week old, tinted stereographs of the mind's eye: bottle-green clumps of New England hills turning lavender in the dusk, flattening to a thousand-mile counterpane of tidy rectangles and squares; non-geometric intersection by the serpentine Missouri; a looming trenchwork of mammoth crags but oddly unreal like spikes of crumpled brown paper thrusting at the plane's belly; those shards of jade-green phosphorescence, the stewardess said, were the swimming pools of Nevada . . .

And now, Darwin said under the pillow, we will discuss in a little more detail the Struggle for Existence.

Shaved, dressed, equipped with bus schedule and street map, he left his junior two rooms on Potrero Hill and entered an elevated, lambent world of air and light, his first fog-free morning since arriving in the legendary city.

September in California, he thought, is not unlike April in Connecticut.

The portal of the Bank of America was appropriately formidable, as was the smiling countenance of the portly officer to whose desk he was shown. *Mr. Horsback* the polished oaken nameplate read.

"A beautiful morning," beamed the owner of this curious appellation.

"Hello. I'd like to open a savings and checking account."

"Splendid. Happy to oblige. If you'll kindly fill out this form . . ."

Jules did so, his glance sporadically reverting to Mr. Horsback as the officer busied himself with an impressive-looking sheaf of papers. The pale eyes, smooth plump face and thinning sandy hair reminded him vividly of Mr. Dillinger, the pharmacist for whom he had worked the summer of his sophomore year at the U. of Connecticut. When answering the phone and being confronted (presumably) with: "Mr. Dillinger? . . ." that genial soul would reply spiritedly, "*I plead guilty!*" Jules' glance fell now to the desk nameplate and he saw what had initially disturbed him.

"Excuse me, but is it possible there's an 'e' missing in your name?"

Mr. Horsback, without raising his eyes, smiled wanly.

An uncanny facsimile of Mr. Dillinger but without the saving grace of humor. Jules slid the completed form across the glass-topped desk.

Shifting the gears of his attention, Mr. Horsback vigorously checked several items with a red pencil. "Will you be depositing directly or transferring funds from another bank?"

"Transferring my entire account from People's Savings in Willimouth, Connecticut," Jules said and felt a compulsion to amplify, " 'Entire account' being a euphemism for two hundred thirty-two dollars and forty cents."

Mr. Horsback judiciously chose to ignore this. "Currently unemployed," he read, then raised his pale eyes and gave Jules a sly off-center smile of collusion. "You have about you the look of an industrious young man bent on changing that status."

You're not intimidating me, Horseback, I refuse to be intimidated.

Smile lingering, the officer strained forward in his chair, head slightly tilted. Jules' lips must have been moving.

"Beg pardon?"

"I intend to seek gainful employment in a matter of hours," Jules said loudly.

Horsback moistened his lips. "Do you have with you your pass book from Weymouth?"

"Willimouth," Jules corrected, handing it over. "A small town, sir, but there are those of us who love it," he added giddily, unable to quell a transitory but ebullient demon.

Hellbent on terminating the interview, Horsback said, "In order to expedite the transfer if you'll sign this authorization—Unless, of course, you prefer to handle the matter personally . . ."

"Lord, no." Jules signed with a flourish. "Only too

happy to shift the weight of responsibility to the broad solvent back of the Bank of California."

"America."

"I beg pardon."

"You mean the Bank of America."

"Of course."

Horsback looked askance at Jules and said, "The transfer will take approximately ten days; we'll be in touch with you. Don't notify us—" he chuckled briefly —"we'll notify you, as the saying goes. Until then . . ." Smiling forcefully, the officer rose and extended a plump hand which Jules warmly clasped. "On behalf of the Bank of America, welcome to California, Mr.—" swift downward glance at the authorization—"Roman, and good luck to you."

"Crazy," Jules said.

Exhilarated, airborne on his newfound freedom, he was in no need of Horsback's thoroughbred felicitations. The day was sundrenched blue and gold, the slender city towers soaring from the hills, a translucent aerie. H. B. Ellis and Irene Bunning light-years distant behind the serpentine Missouri. The gods were beneficent and appeared to be smiling.

Crossing California Street, he was brought out of a half-reverie by an angry squeal of tires and an ear-shattering yell: "*Get with it, Clem!*" A bright red and yellow panel truck careened wildly past him, the driver's ruddy face twisting out the window like some swivel-necked punchinello. What particularly caught Jules' attention, though, inducing a moment's eerie suspension of belief, were the words emblazoned on the receding rear panel: BLIND MAN DRIVING. And a foot below, in slanting unobtrusive script, the annotation: *Pagliacci Venetian Blinds.*

"Marvelous," Jules said aloud.

He spent two dollars for lunch at Blum's Confectionery and over a dish of butterscotch ripple scanned the want ads. Crack salesmen, claims adjusters, merchandise managers, mortgage loan solicitors . . . Teachers: unusual opportunities in experimental educational program, experience with culturally deprived youths in 10–15-year-old bracket. Many thanks, gentlemen; I do sincerely appreciate the opportunity, but I must gratefully, regretfully de— *Personable young man. College education preferred but not necessary. Field interviewer for prominent consumer interest research concern. Car supplied.*

Car supplied.

To his amazement, an hour later, he was hired on the spot. Many thanks, H. B. Ellis. The gods were munificent and smiling steadily.

"You can start immediately if you want," Mr. Mergy, the branch manager, said. "Get in one or two calls before five."

"I think I'll do just that," Jules said. He shook hands with the man and left the office, the manila folder of materials under his arm, the keys to the Plymouth jangling tunefully in his pocket.

Consulting his instruction sheet and a city map, he drove to a specified corner of Van Ness Avenue. An overhead banner proclaimed HARVEY'S USED CARS—BIG DEALS. He got out with his survey sheet attached to a clipboard and looked around for the proprietor.

"Mornin', Jim." A short barrel-shaped man in a green silk shirt and red porkpie hat bore down on him.

Steeping myself in the cultural and historical traditions of this legendary city, Jules remembered with good humor.

"You got the appearance of an intelligent young feller who is in the market for an A-1 vehicle. Is I is or is I ain't right?"

"You isn't," Jules said mildly, the demon still viable.

The man's lunar grin wavered. Eyeing Jules' clipboard, he went on uncertainly, "Yuh, well over here's a job just come in this mornin'. Fifty-six Chevy." A card on the windshield proclaimed: PLENTY MILES IN THE OLD GAL YET: A GORGEOUS CHASSIS. "Sweet little job and clean as a pin." He gave the dark-green hood an authoritative rap with the knuckles. *Paaaaangg.* "You can believe this or no—seventeen thousand miles on 'er from the day she was new."

"I believe you but you've got it all wrong," Jules said. "I represent the Andrew Sylvester Research Company and I have to ask you some questions about gas and oil."

The man's smile collapsed like a bad cake. He regarded Jules obliquely now, head cocked in the manner of a bird dog. "Lemme get this straight. You're not in the market for a car. You're hittin' on Fat Harvey for something."

"It won't take but a moment," Jules said, pencil poised. Another windshield placard grazed the corner of his eye: LOTSA POWER SPELT G-U-T-S. "Do you recommend any particular brand of gasoline to your customers?"

"Jesus, all mornin' nothin' but tirekickers," Fat Harvey sighed, more to himself than aloud. With thumb and forefinger he squeegeed perspiration from his eyes. "Get lost, Jim," he said, walking away.

"It won't cost you anything, just a few minutes of your time . . . I'm only trying to earn a living," Jules called after him.

"You'n me both, baby," Fat Harvey said over his shoulder.

Goddam. I didn't cross the wide Missouri for this kind of treatment, Jules told himself sadly.

It was 4:45. He drove the Plymouth back to Potrero Hill and his junior two rooms. Getting out, he saw across the street like a benign visitation (the gods recompensing for Fat Harvey's loutishness?) a navy-blue Volkswagen, motor revving, a fortyish well-preserved blonde behind the wheel. What struck his eye, though, and sent a quick pang through his heart was not the blonde but the blue and white Connecticut license plate, the first he'd seen in sunny Cal.

He strode across the street and said cheerfully through the open window, "Hi. What town you from?"

The woman gazed at him with wide startled eyes; abruptly the car gave a leap forward, and stalled. Gears grinding, motor whirring again, the terrified little Volks leapt forward a second time and putted nervously away down the hill.

"Crazy," Jules murmured.

In the ground-floor hallway of the apartment house a door quietly opened and Mrs. Williams, his landlady, emerged in her white uniform-dress with the large brass key ring secured to the belt. Oddly she was holding a length of green hose with a shower attachment.

"Mr. Roman, you didn't inform me that you would be using this. Perhaps I should have told you that the use of such attachments is against house rules."

Jules saw now that it was *his* attachment which he'd bought at Newberry's a few days ago.

"Where did you—"

"I was tidying up in your apartment and found your bathroom rug sopping wet. I would guess that it has been in this condition for some days due to the appearance of the linoleum underneath which is beginning to discolor."

"I'd just as soon you didn't enter my rooms to tidy up, Mrs. Williams."

"Mr. Roman, for as long as I've owned this building, I've made a point of periodically inspecting all units." The woman must have moved slightly or quivered, for the keys on the massive ring jangled delicately, tunelessly. When she had first shown him the apartment a week ago, immaculate in her white uniform, trying several keys from the ring before finding the right one, he had had a fleeting semi-fanciful vision of being consigned to a windowless cell, bail rescinded. But the rooms were clean and sunny with bath and kitchen alcove, and the rent, utilities included, seemed reasonable.

"Not only was the linoleum beginning to deteriorate but the pine floor underneath, and quite likely the lath and plaster—"

"Mrs. Williams . . ."

"—and even the joists which support the foundation of the floor. I'm amazed that you would have left a wet rug on the floor all that time. I'm afraid I'll have to hold you responsible for any damages incurred."

"Surely you're joking."

"I most certainly am not."

There was a short thundering silence. Then again the keys jangled tunelessly.

"Are you going to return my shower attachment?" Jules asked in a peremptory manner, hearing, to his dismay, something entreating and forlorn in his voice.

"I'm afraid I'm compelled to confiscate it for as long as you're here."

"Well, Jesus, I don't believe this." He swept past her and up the stairway. "Not for a minute do I believe it," he muttered, letting himself in the apartment, banging the door behind him. Downstairs he heard Mrs. Williams' door close softly, a genteel reproachful echo. In the bathroom, the rug was missing, the linoleum shining where she had evidently mopped up. He hated baths. He'd buy another shower attachment and a bloody double lock for the door. He wouldn't be intimidated. The woman was a monster. Her building or no, there must be a law against entering a room and confiscating private property. Jesus, the goddam bare-faced gall . . .

In the kitchen he sat down and made out his meager time report for Andrew Sylvester Research—a tirekicker that cretin car dealer had called him—entering "Interview incomplete" under Comments. How could the day's fortunes have changed so swiftly? *You're not intimidating me, Fat Harvey, I refuse to be intimidated, baby.*

Then he went to the refrigerator for a beer, changed his mind and dug into a fresh pint of marble fudge.

*   *   *

Late that night Irene Bunning stole soundlessly into his sleep—a taut contained slumber of classroom dimension.

Rarely seeing or hearing her enter, he always knew she was there because the babble stopped on a dime— the rows of baby faces before him suddenly rigid, their collective gaze slanting off to the right.

He thought, turning, My kingdom for a door lock.

"Good evening, Miss Bunning."

The principal looked at him askance. The noon sun was beating against the drawn shades.

"Good morning. Please proceed with your lesson."

Proceed? He could scarcely move.

Bunning, a lank ramrod-straight assortment of bones, wiry coiffure the color of zinc, tiptoed soundlessly down the outside aisle and wedged herself with practiced ease into a rear-desk seat.

Where was he?

On the blackboard he saw in his own handwriting, *The Nile River regularly overflows its banks, providing much needed nourishment for nearby soil.*

"Who can tell me what major city," he addressed the class, "we find at the confluence of the Nile and Missouri?"

Bedlam. Demented laughter booming off the walls.

"You're stupid, Mr. Roman!"

Bunning pursing her lips, with thumb and forefinger rubbing the eyeballs behind rimless spectacles. Unnerved, any haven in a storm, he found himself gazing into the pale-green lovelorn eyes of Christine Dubose. A ten-year-old charmer painted like a Chinatown tart.

Bunning on her feet now, commanding order with a sharp tattoo of the palms. Drawing him out of the front row's hearing range, with an almost impalpable pressure of hand on elbow turning him one hundred eighty degrees so their backs were to the class; he seemed to revolve with fluid frictionless ease like a piston on a crankshaft.

"Would you, Mr. Roman, adhere more closely to your daily lesson plan, which calls for arithmetic third period? Social studies are scheduled for Tuesdays and Thursdays." A voice crackling and virginal, dry as old toast.

Desolate, he studied the limp three-day-dead dwarf dahlias in his desk vase, a gift from the ubiquitous Miss Blassingham.

"I assumed, perhaps wrongly—" summoning his crispest pedantic style—"that the lesson plan was to be used more as a general guide than an inflexible timetable."

Yes, wrongly. Bunning fixing him with a cool intractable eye. Twenty-one-year-old pup of a college boy.

"May I make a suggestion, Mr. Roman?"

"Certainly."

"Would you care to spend the afternoon periods in Miss Blassingham's room while I take over here? I think it might be profitable for you to observe the methods of an experienced teacher."

"Yes, perhaps."

"You understand this is a customary procedure with first-year teachers. No reflection on your ability is intended." There was an overpowering odor of creosote in the room.

"I quite understand."

"Splendid. Good day, Mr. Roman."

"Good night, Irene."

"I beg your pardon."

"I said good night, you miserable old bag."

He came out of it with a thump, rigid, soaking wet, staring dumbly in the dark; where was he?

"Jesus," he thought aloud, "that's too close to home."

Three

Earl Roman taught trigonometry and physical education at Kane Memorial High. His wife had been killed in a motor accident while he was in Korea and he had returned to Willimouth to raise his two sons. A brooding, restless, embittered man, he recited the trigonometric formulae to his class in a rapid singsong litany, *cosinetwoAequalscosinesquaredAminussinesquared A . . . tangenttwoAequalstwotangentAoveroneminus tangentsquaredA*, then impatiently tossed a piece of chalk in the air, catching and tossing it again repeatedly, never missing, while the class recited the incantation back to him. Both Jules and his older brother Arthur, five years apart, had been members of their father's class and had sat numb and dismayed through these daily rituals. Occasionally, if there was time left after the day's formulae had been covered, he would lean back in his swivel chair and relate in an almost wistful way his experiences in past New England track meets when he had run the 220 and 440 hurdles for Springfield College. Only then were his students able to relax, regarding their teacher with a degree of tolerance (and perhaps a glimmer of warmth), forgetting for the moment that they hated his classes and referred to him behind his back, not affectionately, as "Old Cosine Squared."

But in Earl Roman's classes there was never any question of control. At forty-nine he retained the spare sinewy hurdler's physique; something about the bright sunken eyes, sparse silver-gray hair matting his skull like an old cap: a febrile voltaic emanation conveyed itself and as efficaciously as nerve gas paralyzed any potentially rebellious spirits. At the close of his afternoon phys-ed class, Earl Roman would repair to Chief Wehe's Sports Tavern in downtown Willimouth to drink with his cronies and watch whatever sporting events were being televised.

"If Ellis suggested the leave of absence, you can bet your sweet ass Bunning had to be behind it—no pun intended," he said now, continuing the conversation from dinner. "Cunning bastards. A year short of tenure."

Mary, his brother Arthur's wife, had cooked the customary Friday-night fare: pot roast, oven-browned potatoes, peach and cottage cheese salad. It sat rather heavily on Jules' stomach as they adjourned to the living room after the ice-cream-and-cookies dessert.

"A change of venue was the way he put it," Jules said. "To exorcise my *bête noire*."

"What? Your what?"

"The first thing he said when I entered the office was, 'Discipline continues to be our *bête noire*, eh, Mr. Roman?'"

"Good Christ," Arthur said.

As an exercise in mind over personality, Mr. Roman, if you'd assume a sterner, more authoritative demeanor you'd gain the respect of your students. It's as simple—

and difficult—as that.

I've tried, but it seems to go against the grain.

"Jesus, I don't get it. Ten-, eleven-year-old kids. Every day I face boys physically larger and stronger than me and not once in twenty-six years have I ever had to raise my voice."

"The younger kids are a bitch to handle," Arthur said sympathetically. "Come down to the theater on a Saturday morning and see for yourself. It's an experience."

"I think Arthur does amazingly well to keep them under control," Mary said, coming in from the kitchen.

Earl Roman ignored his daughter-in-law and gazed dolefully at his older son. Arthur in six years had had five different jobs; currently he was managing a second-run movie house on the outskirts of Willimouth. "I don't know about you guys," he said vaguely, pouring out more of the port wine he'd brought in from the dining room. "And why California? You have to cross the whole bloody country to take a course in child psychology?"

"Ellis said there's a lot happening in education out there . . . though I don't relish the thought of going back to school. Anyway, I'll get a chance to see California."

"The change of scene will do him good," Arthur said. "And he's free of the Army, that's a break."

Jules winced, wishing his brother would stop being so goddam solicitous.

"You'll have to take some kind of part-time job," his father said. "Make up your mind about that."

"Okay," Jules said, letting out his breath. Old Cosine Squared. A quarter century of trigonometry and locker rooms. How had he got through it?

There was a silence broken by two words from Mary, sitting across the room, hefty legs tucked under her, perusing the *World Almanac*: "Outerbridge Horsey."

The three men stared at her. She looked up, her plump face flaming slightly under the scrutiny. "Our ambassador to Czechoslovakia. His name is Outerbridge Horsey."

"We're talking family problems, baby," Arthur said.

Mary: a grand old name, Jules thought. *And there is something there that sounds so square.*

"All the courses in the world aren't going to help," his father said. "You know that."

"I guess. Mind over personality."

"Discipline's only one factor," Arthur said. "Why, Jule has more going for him intellectually than most—"

"Intellectually, balls. He's teaching ten-year-old babies. Are those wet-nurse biddies in the other classrooms all Nobel geniuses, for Christ's sake? What's intellectually got to do with it? If he hasn't got command of his class in front, he might as well try to teach a goddam brick wall." Earl tilted the port bottle to pour the remaining few inches into his glass, most of it sloshing onto the coffee table, dripping to the beige rug.

"Father, I think we've had about enough," Mary scolded, crossing the room to take the bottle out of his hand.

And there is something there that sounds so square.

"Stop fussing around, you little beanbag, and bring us another bottle," Earl said, and whacked her heartily and lovingly on her fat little behind. The rest of Mary froze but that round bottom seemed to oscillate for seconds afterward. Mouth crimped, crimson to the ears, she proceeded primly to the kitchen.

"I don't know, maybe I made a mistake with you guys," Earl went on, pensive now. "I suppose I could've married again, haven't enjoyed myself much. But you always ate well, plenty of exercise and fresh air. I never shielded you from an honest fight. No place along the line I can see where I went wrong . . ." Their father's speech was thickening and Jules and Arthur exchanged a brief look over his head. Before their eyes now he seemed to sink in on himself, sighing hoarsely, slumping lower in the stuffed chair, gaunt hands folded over the concavity of his chest. He looked from one to the other with distant, sorrowful, glazed eyes. Now his gaze dropped to the floor and he spoke softly, ruefully, as if to himself. "Goddam, what goes with you guys anyway."

Jules felt his heart contract and shrivel inside him. He closed his eyes for a moment, abruptly shook his head like a dog coming out of water. "Mary," he called loudly into the kitchen, "is there any more ice cream?"

Four

Carmel Brown, age twenty, drove from St. Helena to San Francisco in her '49 sedan with the emergency brake on all the way, smelling the burning leather smell but not connecting it with the brake, accustomed to odd noises, smells, and malfunctions, hunched forward, accelerator jammed to the floor, thinking resignedly, This shitbox gonna konk out any minute now.

But she made it to the City and chugged into a Texaco station.

"A dollar's worth of regular and can you tell me what that smell is."

The attendant checked, told her, and suggested she leave the car for a couple of hours.

"My suitcase and other things is in the back. All I own."

"They'll be safe, Miss."

"Is it a far walk to North Beach?" She had been told the Beach was a place where dark and light folk met and commingled with ease. Longwell might be there.

"You turn right on Broadway, then about a half mile straight on," said the attendant, a look of troubled yearning on his face.

In her city clothes and high heels, carrying her big

wicker bag, she started out, her face as stark and grave and contained as an Indian's, the thin limber body held straight, unconsciously feline. Along Broadway a number of people turned to look after her—women as well as men—with varied expressions but all somehow allied to the station attendant's wistfulness. They couldn't know—the passers-by and motorists—that she was silently, theatrically exhorting herself, "C'mon, feet, do yo' duty." Miss Stepin' Fetchit Brown.

Nee Caramel (sic) by an antic octoroon mother who thought she'd come out lighter than she did; over the years, naturally, blessedly, it shortened to Carmel. The five of them—including her father, Julius, a maintenance worker for the Manor Motel, an older half sister, Raven, and a brother, Longwell, of indeterminate ancestry (conceived, Mrs. Brown thought, though unsure of *which* night, in the back seat of a car parked on Longwell Road)—lived in a four-room two-story clapboard house on the outskirts of St. Helena.

The three children slept in one room and Carmel's most graphic memory of the old house was the night Longwell came in late when the girls were already in their bed and said as he was undressing in the dark, "Hey, I know something feels good." The girls giggled and Longwell said from across the room, "Raven, hey, come on over." Carmel, stuffing knuckles in her mouth, still giggling, said, "I'm gonna tell." "It's something real good," Longwell pressed. "You go on to sleep," Raven said, turning over on her side. Longwell, out of his clothes and in bed, began whistling a leisurely tune, nonchalant. "You don't know whatcher missing." He kept on with the whistling and as Carmel was snuggling into sleep, she felt her sister slip out from under the covers. Wide-eyed in the darkness, holding her breath to bursting, she strained to hear the muffled voices across the room. Abruptly the voices stopped, there was a harsh rustling sound of sheets and blankets—a high thin giggle from Raven—then nothing but the rustling sounds. Long minutes later Longwell started whistling again and Raven slipped back into bed. "What was it?" Carmel whispered, frantic. "Nothing." Her sister turned over. "*What was it?*" She began pummeling Raven's back with her tiny fists, pumping her knees rapidly against her sister's legs as if she were riding a bicycle. "It wasn't anything, go to sleep," Raven said irritably. Across the room Longwell snickered, then let loose a series of loud hee-haw noises like a donkey. "I'm gonna tell!" Carmel wailed. "You do and you'll get a bust in the mouth," Longwell told her. Whimpering, she thrashed around for another minute or two; then, as no one paid her any attention, she gradually subsided and cried herself softly to sleep. A half dozen times in the following weeks she felt Raven slip out of bed in response to Longwell's whistling, listened to the rustling of her nightie and the sound of her bare feet padding across the floor. She would bury her head under the pillow and start thrashing, pummeling her absent sister with her knees and fists, trying to drown everything out. She came to dread the nights. Finally she told her mother she couldn't fall asleep with Raven in the same bed and begged her to let her sleep on the sofa in the parlor. Concerned over the girl's continued loss of appetite, the puckered hollows under her eyes, her mother agreed. That was the year Carmel was seven,

Longwell ten, and Raven a blooming pubescent twelve.

The Browns were one of the few colored families in St. Helena and Carmel the only Negro in her class at school. An average student (except for her spelling, which was atrocious), tormented in devious ways by her classmates, she made friends with an obese ginger-haired girl named Francine Fisher. Francine Fatty, her classmates called her, and they nicknamed her bosom buddy Charcoal Brown. The girls presented an irresist-ible target, one fat and fair-skinned, the other dark and scarecrow-thin with immense brown eyes giving her narrow face a speckled haunting mournful look. The two names became a kind of watchword; the other chil-dren took to saying to one another in tenuous moods of boredom or anger or glee—sometimes for no tangible reason at all—"Francine Fatty 'n' Charcoal Brown." A boy yawning in the midst of a deadly geography lesson might lean forward and murmur to the pupil in front of him, "Francine Fatty 'n' Charcoal Brown." The girls grew steadfast and inseparable in their mutual estrange-ment, meeting the taunts with a shaky arrogance and rebel pride, sticking out their tongues and giving their tormentors the bird, then giggling wildly and fleeing hand in hand across the schoolyard. Soon they were flaunting their ostracism like a badge. After school they did their homework together, usually at Francine's house, where there was a 16-inch TV in the parlor. They watched the late-afternoon movies, mimicking the actors and taking off on situations of their own devising, Francine the highfalutin mistress of the house repri-manding Carmel as the shiftless, no-account or imperti-nent-type maid (now Butterfly McQueen, now Hattie

McDaniel), improvising costumes with sequins and beads and bits of lace and ribbon. They read each other's palms and exchanged accounts of the previous night's dreams. Carmel had recently discovered an ability to *control* her dreams, at least most of the time. During nightmare sequences when the dread footsteps approached outside the door or the fat beady-eyed little man stalked her with the monstrous club, she calmly instructed herself, "Wake up. Wake up, wake up . . ." And it seemed always to happen before the club struck or the footsteps could be followed by a savage pounding on the door. Several times a week she was able to fashion the dream wherein she suddenly had money to spare, more than enough to taxi into town and buy a certain blue-and-green harlequin-pattern dress in Hanley's store window, trying it on, having the smiling saleslady lay it lovingly on the bed of tissue in the box and actually wearing it at a party that same night before the dream dissolved and it was morning. But there was one recurrent dream which she found she had less control over: the nude, sad-eyed, penisless little boy who suddenly materialized in front of her while she was curled up in a chair, reading; she'd peek over the top of the book, wary, and he'd always be there, but she couldn't move, her body was glued to the chair; the boy stood very close, staring up into her face in a quiet, doleful way and when she tried to tell herself, "Wake up, wake up," her jaw was gummed shut, the words wouldn't form. All in all, though, she was quite pleased with her nocturnal skill. Sometimes she'd come awake mornings on the parlor sofa and find her mother staring down at her. "Now what're you talkin' about?"

"Huh. . .?"

"You been mumblin' away, goin' on senselessly."

"The man was comin'. . ."

"Get up and get dressed. Francine's here."

Francine retained her fat over the years—her obesity had been traced to an affliction called primary hyper-aldosteronism—and she and Carmel remained insepa-rable friends through their second year in high school. That year they regularly attended the school dances which were held the last Saturday of every month in the gymnasium. They got all gussied up in glittery dresses of their own creation and sat patiently in the bleachers waiting for the cut-in dances to be announced. When the time came they emerged from the bleachers hand in hand and each picked out a boy; then, at a prearranged signal over their partners' shoulders (the boys holding them at arm's length, grimacing with distaste), they would give the boys a rude shove backward, break away and race wildly up into the bleachers, flinging over their shoulders, "Dumb dodo!" "Jerk!" "Shithead!" Remi-niscing the next day, they agreed it was the best fun they could ever remember having, and recalling the ex-pressions on the boys' faces, they would break up for days afterward.

But at the close of the sophomore year Francine's family moved to Oregon; it was the last Carmel ever saw of her friend.

For her birthday that year her mother gave her an embossed leather-jacketed autograph album with alter-nating cinnamon, yellow and mauve pages. Unable to think of anyone around St. Helena whose autograph she wanted (she would have liked on the first cinnamon page: To my best friend—Francine "Fatty" Fisher), she began jotting down fragmentary thoughts and short poetry-like descriptions of her more bizarre dreams, which she always remembered vividly, even two or three days later. She took out a book from the library, *Spiritual Gratification Through Dream Analysis*, and read through it absorbedly, laboring over the passages she didn't understand. It helped fill the painful void left by Francine's departure.

The autograph album was the last thing her mother ever gave her, for she died that winter, and Julius Brown used the insurance money as down payment on the El Rancho Cottages, a somewhat dilapidated motel complex of six units which he'd had his eye on for a long time. The Cottages catered to the transient workers (many of dubious character and volatile temperament) in the vineyards around St. Helena and had changed hands a number of times in the past few years, most likely because of sporadic police harassment. Well aware of this stigma, Julius changed the name to Morpheus Ranch Cottages and thought that by a general improvement in the physical appearance and gingerly screening of the clientele (weeding out the drunks and obvious baddies in front, leaving "the more fit of the Caucasian trade" as he put it) he could placate the Forces of Law and Order, if, hopefully, they were inclined to be placated. Then by having Carmel do the bulk of the cleaning work, there was a good chance of a steady if modest profit. During the past two years the family had spread out. Longwell had gone to San Francisco to look for work and Raven was working as a live-in maid for one of the big winery families, leaving her baby, Jo-jo (not Longwell's; that activity had ceased ages ago), in Carmel's care.

So it happened at the first of the new year that Julius, Carmel, and Jo-jo moved into the rear two rooms of the largest cottage, reserving the front part as an office. A spanking bright neon sign jutted up from the ridge of the newly shingled roof

MORPHEUS RANCH COTTAGES

GAS

OIL

SANDWICHES

and with the six units forming an approximate semi-circle about the single gas pump, a veritable rainbow-view of fresh pastel colors was afforded the motorists on Route 29.

With the burden of caring for Jo-jo, cleaning the cottages, changing the bedding, and selling the plastic-wrapped sandwiches from the rack on the front-room counter, Carmel was forced to quit school midway through her junior year. Still thin, but with a natural suppleness about her movements now, the dark eyes grown enormous in a silent, sweet, expressionless face, she was surprised (being unaware of the change) to find two or three of the boys from her high school dropping by for gas and lingering to talk to her. They no longer called her Charcoal, and before long one and then another were asking her out to the local Drive-In. She would have liked just watching the movie, then going someplace for a Coke or Calso and talking about school, which she missed, and her dreams, or, better, to the Club Napa on the road to Lake Hennessey where there was a band and a white girl who was said to sound like Billie Holiday. (She wondered why they never took her to the club or into town, though she thought she knew.) Invariably, after the film started, the boy would slide over on the seat, his lips brushing her ear and cheek and neck, nervous hands roaming the upper part of her body. She shied away, still trying to watch the movie, making whimpering, deprecatory sounds in the midst of which the boy might detect a plaintive, mumbled, "I'm gonna tell" and, when the lips and hands persisted, "Listen, I can't do nothin'." If the going got really serious, a hand clamping on one of her breasts or starting under her skirt, she'd whimper in a drawn-out breathy monotone, "Owowowowowowowow." This usually had the effect of infuriating the boy, and when further grappling proved futile, he'd either sit out the movie in a black sulk or, more often, exasperated by the waste of an evening, sullenly put the car in gear and drive her home. When she was let out at the gas pump she'd say, "I'm sorry I can't do nothin', are you still my friend?. . . Don't I get to see you again?" She didn't get to see him again, and after a while no more boys were dropping by for gas.

Meanwhile she was putting away the ten dollars her father gave her every week, for she had made up her mind (though she hadn't yet told him) that she was eventually going to leave St. Helena. Now that Francine was gone there was nothing to keep her here. She wasn't going to spend her life making other people's beds—Julius would have to find himself another housemaid; and though she loved Jo-jo and hated the thought of leaving him, that was Raven's red wagon and some other arrangements (she prayed the little tyke wouldn't be taken away to one of those institutions with high walls and barred windows) would have to be made. What she'd do, she'd buy herself a second-hand jalopy and go to San Francisco—get a real job, a career—and try to find Longwell, who hadn't even written once since he'd left more than a year ago.

The drudgery of the daily cleaning was really getting to her. She found it went easier if she talked to herself, mimicking the movie domestics, making enervated no-rest-for-the-weary charwoman sounds. "Ooooee, mmmh . . . Lordy, me back's cavin'. This ol' broom weigh two ton if it weigh a pound . . . Uhhhn. Got to keep on keepin' on . . . 'Carmel, dear, have you polished the silver yet?' "—a smooth change of inflection here— "Yes'm, Miz Rockefeller, I's gettin' to that presently . . . Ahhh, mmmh. Lord, I gets weary, I jus' don't know where I finds the strength . . . Unnhhh . . ." Once she stopped in mid-incantation to find her father gazing stupefied in at her through the screened window. For a couple of seconds they stared silently at each other.

"Baby's cryin'," her father said finally.

"Okay, Julius," she said, putting down the broom.

Jo-jo slept in the small back room with her and she loved to kiss and fondle and mother him. "How's Mammy's baby, mmmh? How *is* he?. . . Is your pants dry? Is they?—Ecchhhh. Mammy's gonna bite your face, Chicken Little. She's gonna bite it right off . . ." Late at night when she heard the soft mournful cooing cry, "Waadoo, waadoo . . ." she'd slide out of bed, still half asleep, moving trancelike to get him a glass of water. And as she propped him up, her hand supporting the fat little neck, and got the edge of the glass in his mouth, she'd murmur soothingly, mimicking the baby-sound, "Waadoo, waadoo." She truly loved Jo-jo.

The Cottages were doing all right, not flourishing as they say, but operating at enough capacity so that Julius was able to meet his monthly payments. The cops dropped by twice, leisurely looked around and, seemingly satisfied, left, smilingly refusing Julius' offer to take a half-dozen sandwiches home "for the kiddies or a nighttime fam'ly snack." Now and then one of the vineyard workers would linger in the front office to talk to Carmel, asking her what she did for excitement, or, half banteringly, "How's about you and me going grape-picking tonight?" "Thanks, but I's nevah had much taste fo' the grape," Carmel would answer in her deliberate down-home lingo, going about her business. Julius kept as close an eye as possible on the situation, murmuring ominously to himself, "The Caucasians is in heat today," and one night at supper spoke to her about it, forbidding her to have anything to do with the men beyond "common everyday business transactions 'n' the like." Truth was, after her experiences at the Drive-In, she couldn't have been less inclined.

She spent her evenings watching old movies on the small TV set which the previous owner had sold them —the older the better, savoring the more antic minor character roles—and from time to time, during dull passages or lengthy commercials, jotting scraps of poetry on the varicolored pages of the autograph album that she always kept by her side. She used fifteen dollars of the money she was saving to buy a secondhand portable phonograph and every night before going to bed she sang along (very softly so as not to wake Jo-jo) with Ella Fitzgerald or Lena Horne or Billie Holiday (Billie's "Miss Brown to You" understandably her favorite), and occasionally, for broadening, equalitarian purposes, Peggy Lee and Anita O'Day. She thought it would be nice if someday she became a torch singer in a night club.

One Saturday afternoon a man who had been staying in the cottage named Columbine for almost a week—not a vineyard worker but a man selling some kind of machinery in the St. Helena–Rutherford–Oakville area —asked her if she'd like to visit one of the wineries with him. She'd spoken to him a few times and he always looked oddly familiar to her, as if she'd seen him somewhere before (which wasn't likely; she'd never *been* anywhere), a short plump balding man with baby-smooth skin and small kindly pale-blue eyes. Mr. Saunders was his name.

"Well, see, I can't leave the baby," Carmel said.

"How about that girl who comes around?" He meant Margarita, the Portuguese girl who lived a half mile down the road and sometimes helped Carmel with the cleaning or looked after Jo-jo.

"I s'pose I could call her. I never been to the wineries."

"There's a tour where they show you how it's made from the grapes and you can choose any kind of wine you want to drink, free," Mr. Saunders said. "Why don't you call the girl."

She did. Margarita wasn't home.

"Guess I'll have to go myself then," Mr. Saunders said, smiling, and went back to his cottage.

The next afternoon he said he hadn't got around to it yesterday and asked again if she'd like to go. Margarita was home this time and said she could come, but only for a couple of hours. They went to tell her father. Julius frowned and rubbed his nose, looking the man over. "For an old feller like me it's nice to have company on a tour," Mr. Saunders said, smiling in a pallid but friendly way.

Julius rubbed his nose again. "You be back for supper," he said to Carmel.

" 'Course I will. Somebody got to cook, don't they?"

Mr. Saunders drove toward one of the wineries, then left the main highway and drove along a paved road bordering the fields. "We'll come in the back way. I want you to see the whole layout." He turned onto a dirt road and then into a rutted path that stopped shortly at a construction of boards on which a No Trespassing sign was crudely lettered in white paint.

"I thought we was goin' to the winery," Carmel said, uneasy.

"There's plenty of time."

Mr. Saunders lit a cigarette, and as he smoked, looking straight ahead through the windshield, his pudgy hand fell carelessly on her knee. Carmel edged back against the door. "I'm gonna tell . . ." She dearly wished she were back playing with Jo-jo or writing in her album; and there was the cleaning still to be done in the Wisteria Cottage. Mr. Saunders removed his hand and slowly, deliberately, ground out the cigarette in the ashtray. Finally he turned to her, smiling—but something was wrong with the smile. Now as he moved laboriously from beneath the wheel toward her, she saw the tiny pearls of sweat on his upper lip and forehead, and the small pale eyes seemed to grow smaller, shrinking like raisins.

"Don't you want to be nice to me? There's no harm in being nice to an old man, is there?"

As the pudgy hand fell again on her bare knee and slipped under the tight cotton skirt, Carmel, eyes huge with fright, suddenly saw why he had looked familiar: the beady eyes and fat sweaty face belonged to the man in her dream who stalked her with the club. *Wake up, wake up,* she whispered to herself. The stubby fingers were scrabbling up her thigh like the appendages of some loathsome creature.

"I can't do nothin'," she whimpered.

"You know where my finger's going." Mr. Saunders' voice was soft, toneless.

"Naw. Let's go to the winery." The door handle was jabbing painfully into her back.

"I'll rotate it around. Warm you up."

"Naw. Please. Let's go t' the winery."

"You're going to like it."

"Owowowowowowow," Carmel whimpered.

Then Mr. Saunders was all over her, thrashing about and making terrible guttural noises, the sweat dripping off his smooth round face onto her blouse.

The rape was accomplished—though in the cramped conditions of the front seat barely successfully—and Carmel was back in plenty of time to fix supper.

The next morning Mr. Saunders checked out.

"I thought he was figuring to stay on to Wednesday," Julius said.

"Yeah. So did I."

Carmel never told anyone, and when she thought about it during the next few days she blinked and gave her head a shake and told herself, "It's just unbelievable." Once or twice in bed she clenched her teeth and pummeled the mattress with her fists and knees. The old fart. Pow! She should have given it to him right in his fat flabby face. Then after another week she ceased thinking about it altogether. And oddly enough she stopped having the dream about the man with the club.

Six months later—Margarita ensconced in the back room with Jo-jo—she piled her worldly belongings in a 1949 sedan and, equipped with a driver's license issued by an overkindly inspector, took off for the City.

Five

Now, entering San Francisco's North Beach (which is not a beach at all, she discovered), all the time keeping an eye peeled for Longwell and wishing Francine was with her, she paused before a night-club entrance, gazing at the inset photograph of an enticingly coiffed and gowned blonde bombshell, copious cleavage and an appealing hoydenish smile. The legend underneath read: Hurry to Get an Eyeful and an Earful of a Swinger Destined for the Very Top in Show Biz.

"Everything's gonna be just everything," Carmel said softly to no one in particular.

She stopped at a newsstand and bought a paper. Diagonally across the street was a likely-looking place—Dante's Excelsior Coffeehouse—to get her bearings and rest her feet, and she entered, hesitant, squinting into the gloom. Trying to ignore the glances directed her way, she settled at a table in the window alcove where there was light to read by and opened the paper, scanning the want-ad pages for night-club singers. There was no such category. Someone was standing over her; she looked up into the pallid face of a lank-haired white girl in black stockings, black skirt and sweater. The girl was smiling, waiting for her order.

"Ah think ah'll try me some o' that *espresso*," Carmel said, for some reason lapsing into her down-home dialect. And as the girl turned to go: "Uh, Miss . . ."

"Jean."

"Jean. Okay. I'm lookin' for a Longwell Brown. He's my brother."

"The name doesn't ring a bell."

"I think he's here in this area somewhere."

"I'll ask around."

Jean returned with the espresso, accompanied by a tall rough-skinned man with a thick reddish-blond beard, dressed in jeans and a lumber jacket. The man straddled a chair, resting his chin on his hands along the back, peering intently at Carmel.

"Who you looking for?"

"My brother Longwell," Carmel said, shrinking back just a little under the scrutiny.

"I don't bite. Where'd you come from?"

"Up north. St. Helena."

"And you're looking for your brother. If you don't find him you'll need a place to stay."

"Well, yeah . . ."

The man said nothing for a moment; his gaze was intense, almost demonic, the light-blue eyes under coarse blond brows glittering like mica. Carmel tried to keep on looking at him and felt a throbbing begin at the back of her skull.

"I have a couple Johns who might be interested. You got eyes?"

"Huh?"

The man flicked his beard with a paint-stained knuckle. "Never mind."

"Ah'm just lookin' for my brother Longwell and a place to stay and maybe a singin' job," Carmel said in a rush.

The man kept on looking at her.

"O'Hara," a girl said behind him. She was dressed like the waitress Jean, but considerably older, squat and fleshy-faced with heavy round breasts bulging beneath a shapeless sweater.

Without turning, the man stood up. "There's a place called Havila Apartments two blocks from here on Pacific. It's integrated and low rent if that's what you're looking for."

"That does sound like what I'm lookin' for," Carmel avowed.

The man rapped his stained knuckles on the chair back and abruptly joined the big-breasted girl. "You're crowding me, Dori," Carmel heard him say as they walked toward the back of the room. Vaguely upset by the encounter, she turned now and looked out the window at the passers-by—young people mostly, sloppily dressed and unclean-looking, the girls with long straggly hair and no make-up; something vacant and aimless about them. Not one of them, she thought, would you be likely to see on the tidy tree-shaded streets of St. Helena. Finishing her coffee, she folded up the newspaper, opened her wicker bag and took out her autograph album; stared out the window for another minute or two, then opened to a fresh mauve page and entered a few lines. Scowling slightly at what she had written, she eased her shoes off under the table and supplely arched her back, rubbing the small of it with her left hand and whispering with a harsh, rasping inflection,

"Aieee tu-tu-tu-tu-tu-tu, shore 'n' the deevil be havin' me back afore the fortnight." Barry Fitzgerald Brown.

The next morning Carmel awakened in her low-rent two rooms in the Havila Apartments and stared for minutes at the unfamiliar calcimined ceiling. Since the days when her mother had caught her mumbling sense-lessly in the mornings, she had made it a point, on com-ing awake, to shut off the aftermath of whatever dream she'd been having, collect her thoughts and express them rationally, aloud.

"I got to get up. Face life. Face the nation."

The man at the Texaco station hadn't had time to fix her car yesterday and she'd had to take a taxi back to the apartment, lugging her phonograph and the wicker bag filled with toilet articles. This morning she'd have to go on back there again.

It was cold in the apartment, colder than fall in St. Helena. Leery of the oddly shaped gas heater (she'd heard whole families could be asphyxiated by one), she tried to light the oven broiler with matches, found the gas outlets illogically distant and finally managed it using a furled page of yesterday's newspaper as a torch.

She put on her Billie Holiday LP and got back into bed with the want-ad section, scanning the headings until she came to *Household Help: Women*. She cir-cled several entries with a pencil, then lay back and pulled the covers up around her neck, echoing Lady Day in a shaky contralto:

> *Who d'you think is comin' to town*
> *You'll never guess who*

Lovable, hug-able Emily Brown
Miss *Brown to you*

Wha' do I care if the rain comes down
My heaven is blue

She stopped singing and pulled the covers up tighter. "I got to keep on keepin' on," she said.

The new brake lining cost thirteen dollars, and the attendant, who had made a few other temporary adjustments free of charge, advised her to dump the car.

"I just bought it a couple months back."

"I'm afraid you made a bad buy. It's on its last legs, Miss. I wouldn't drive it much longer."

"Its last wheels I guess you mean," Carmel said.

The attendant regarded her dumbly for a moment, then began laughing wildly, nervously, inordinately. He ran a grease-stained hand over his cropped head.

"Last wheels—of course. That's funny. . . ."

The attendant was right as rain. An hour later, just as she was cresting Union Street on her way to an interview, the shitbox done konked out on her for good.

Six

His fifth day on the job with Andrew Sylvester Research Inc. Jules was transferred from Fuel and Oil Products (Wave I) to the Household Interest Survey.

"No reflection on your ability," Mr. Mergy said (it took Jules but a second to recall where he'd heard that precise phrase before). "Simply we feel your type of personality would be better suited to the household interviews. Car dealers are rough nuts to crack," he added, and left Jules alone to peruse the instruction sheets.

PURPOSE OF THE SURVEY: *To study people's interests in magazines and radio programs. You will show the people you interview items in several magazine issues, page by page, to find out which items look especially interesting to them, and whether or not they have looked into the issue before. You will ask these people questions about radio: what radio stations and programs do they prefer, which ones do they listen to most often?, etc.*

DON'T SKIP ANY HOUSEHOLDS: *When counting and interviewing you must include every household on your assigned path of "blue arrows." No place is too poor, dirty, or shabby. The poor shabby house-*

holds will provide the most important consumer-sociological information in this survey. . . .

With foreboding he read on:

If a rural-appearing lane turns off the main road at one of your locations, go all the way down it to the end—it could lead to a farmhouse or shack. Whatever people live on the lane, don't skip them. In fact make a special effort *with these people, for in many respects they are the most valuable. Don't overlook any kind of dwelling if anyone at all lives there. Be sure to include non-white as well as white households.*

Watch particularly for small houses behind large houses, apartments above or behind stores. If there's a poor family living in a shack off in the woods, get them. If there's an Indian family in a teepee, or a Mexican family in a brush hut, get them. . . .

"How're you coming along?" Mr. Mergy said, returning.

"Indian family in a teepee . . ."

"Exaggeration for effect. The point is, there's a temptation to skip the darkies and other off-color races in a borderline area. If you don't cover every household on your assignment, the cross-section won't be valid. *Comprends?*"

"I understand," Jules said.

"Your main obstacle is convincing the respondent in front that you're not *selling* the magazines. That's the purpose of the pocket-flash gift. Token of good faith. You're giving *them* something. If you still have trouble, present the Better Business Bureau leaflet."

"I see."

"Finish reading the instructions, organize your material. Then out in the field with you, Roman!" With a bonny wink and a grin, Mergy slapped Jules smartly on the shoulder and breezed out of the office.

The first door he knocked on was a ground-floor apartment in the Bayview district. A balding man in a frayed terrycloth bathrobe opened the door.

"Good morning. We're conducting a survey to find what magazine items most inter—"

"Nothing doing."

"I'm not selling them. If you'll accept this—"

"Beat it."

The door closed in his face.

FUCK MR ROMAN he remembered crudely lettered in blue chalk across the front walk of the school building at eight in the morning. Running, mortified, with a furtive glance over her shoulder, awkwardly trying to expunge it with the sole of her brogue.

Mrs. Gloria Johnson, the nameplate on the door of Apt. 2 read. *Sic transit gloria mundi.* His last half year at the U. of Conn. Gloria, a non-resident Kappa Alpha Theta with an apartment off campus. In her tub shower, water streaming down the glazed curtain decorated with court jesters, they soaped each other's bodies; Gloria, eyes beryl-bright, bombed on martinis, *Okay, Roman, I think that's enough on that particular spot that'll do just fine thank you Roman* back to back bumping asses singing *Lavender blue dilly* bump *Lavender green, When I am* bump *dilly dilly You shall be queen* . . . Good long while before he'd forget Miss Gloria Deitweiler '64. Used to think if he didn't get laid for another five years he could live on the memory of those six months. Drank like a fish *Roman apply ice-cold wash cloth to back of neck can't make love in this condition. Yes, thank you. Now. Friend Roman countryman lend me your cock. Lollipop time* and a week after graduation married her history instructor. *Sic transit gloria mundi.*

With trepidation he tapped on the door. And was about to turn away when it opened. A hefty colored woman, hair whitening, dubiously regarded the magazines under his arm.

"Ain't got any money an' don't need 'em."

"I'm not selling anything. I'm making a survey. Here, this is for you. Free." Jules proffered the gilded pocket flashlight.

"Well you come on in here where I can get a look at you."

Jules followed her in. "I'm just makin' some tea. There's another cup 'n' saucer in that cupboard."

He drew a long steadying breath, blinking with relief. Had his arms been free at the moment he would have humbly hugged the old woman in gratitude.

It took him five hours to cover the entire building: seven acceptances, three doors in the face, two partially completed interviews. He drove home dry-mouthed and exhausted, wondering how long he could continue in this particular vocation. (*After careful consideration, Mr. Mergy, and no little introspection, I've arrived at the sad conclusion, sir, that I'm really not built for this type of work*.) Courage. In front of his apartment house he hopefully looked again for the navy-blue Connecticut Volks. The woman had been understandably frightened the way he'd rushed at her that day and he was sure that she'd turn out to be a genial soul once she learned that he too was a down-home alumnus of the Constitution State. But the Volks was nowhere in sight; he had the feeling he'd never see it again.

On his kitchen table was the freshly cleaned bathroom rug and, pinned to it, a note:

Mr. Roman:

Clean & dry bathroom rug	$ .75
General damage to linoleum, joists &	
plaster by shower spray	7.00
To be applied to this month's rent.	
	$ 7.75

Thank you,
Mrs. Williams, Mgr.

God, the woman was larcenous, an out-and-out thief. He'd have to begin seriously looking for a new place. He checked the bedroom closet to see if his new shower attachment was still in its hiding place. Having to conceal his own property! And carefully sponging the floor now after every bath—intimidated again! She could have easily left the note and rug outside the door. A double lock was probably futile; she'd find some way of confiscating that, too, attacking with screwdriver and hatchet if necessary, a latter-day Carry Nation, sanctioned by infringement of house rules. The vicious old bag. Doubtless a distant kin of Irene Bunning's. He was beginning to hear that massive jangling ring of keys in his sleep. One thing was for damn sure—she'd have to wait for another coming of the Messiah before she'd see that $7.75.

After making out his time report, scarcely cheered to find that he had earned $11.45 for the day, he took from his wallet a worn and much-folded note composed by one Mrs. Wasserman, formerly Cora Mayberry, who, after thiry-one years in the teaching profession, had retired to get married. It was this vacancy he had filled at Weaver St. School. The note had made the rounds of all the rooms and had come to him last "for perusing and disposal" as Bunning phrased it in an inter-class memo concerning such trivia.

My dear Friends on the Weaver St. Faculty,

    What a delicious surprise it was for me to receive your chic and thoughtful gift. How can I ever thank you enough for these exquisite gloves? They are long, black, and extremely swish, and my husband thinks I look quite Parisienne in them!

    May you all stay well and someday encounter the good fortune which has befallen me.

        I bless you,

        Cora Mayberry Wasserman

P.S. "Chuck" says hello to each and every one of you!

Whenever he was feeling low he took out the note and read it. It always cracked him up a little, raised his spirits. God bless you too, Cora.

Now he looked out the window at the gathering dusk, the first lights gleaming palely in the distant Nob

Hill hotels. A towering blue-black fog was moving in from the ocean. The evening yawned ahead of him.

> *Lavender blue, dilly dilly*
> *Lavender green*
> *If I were king . . . dilly dilly*

Seven

Jules emerged from the Union Street residence buoyant, an unaccustomed mood of late. He'd just completed his third consecutive successful interview of the morning. The gilded pocket flashlight was working like a charm. And the radio part of the interview was going quickly and smoothly; simply no one ever seemed to listen to it any more (unless in a car and that didn't count). After laying the flash on Mrs. Rautenberg, he'd been home free, coming out of it with coffee and Danish in the bargain.

I'll tackle a hausfrau over a bloody car dealer any day in the week, he thought, eyeing the junk heap backed at a precarious angle against the curb. The girl peering dubiously under the hood made his breath catch. With that sweet grave face and those dark soulful eyes she looked like a dusky Madonna.

"Hi, what's the trouble?"

"Life done dealt me another blow," Carmel sighed. "My jalopy's fritzed out again."

Knowing next to nothing about engines, Jules got in and tried starting it.

"It might be your battery. Do you have Triple A?"

"Huh?"

"They have a towing service. I wouldn't leave it like

this if I were you. You're blocking traffic."

"I was on my way to a interview. A secre*tarial* position." The serenity of Carmel's expression just perceptibly altered now, a faint elfin disturbance rippling the somber features like the flicker of light on still water.

This subtle change affected Jules inordinately. "I have a little free time. I could drive you there, then use my Triple A card and have your jalop—car towed to a station."

"You would? Would you do that for me?" The big dark eyes almost undid him.

"Yes. Of course."

Jules slipped a hasty note—*Emergency: broken down, in the process of attending to*—under the windshield wiper and they got into the Plymouth.

"I'm Jules Roman."

"That's like my old man's name. Julius."

"And you're—"

"Carmel Brown. Miss Brown to you."

He turned to her. "Really?"

"Naw, it's just an expression."

"Where to, Carmel?"

She poked around in her wicker bag and found the address.

They had driven about five blocks when Jules suddenly went to the accelerator and pulled alongside the slow-moving car in front of him, lightly tapping his horn to get the driver's attention. He leaned across Carmel and called out the window, "Hi, what town you from?"

The aged Chinaman in the black Chrysler with Connecticut plates turned slowly, regarding him with impenetrable Oriental calm.

"Jesus, I don't get it," Jules murmured, pulling past the Chrysler.

"How will I know where my jalopy's at?" Carmel said, on a track of her own.

"Is there a station near where you live?"

"Ah don't recollect. Wait . . ." She rummaged in the bag again, came up with the card given her by the man who had replaced her brake lining

TEXACO SERVICE

WE GIVE S & H GREEN STAMPS

Mario Salvato   *Cor. Van Ness and Pacific*

and handed it to Jules.

A few minutes later he turned into Jackson Street. The address for the job interview turned out to be an impressive ivy-covered two-story edifice. "Is this it—a house?"

"Yeah," Carmel said, regretting her secretarial fabrication.

"Call me later about the car." He scribbled his number on a slip of paper. "I'll be home after five."

She took it and got out, coming around to his window and fixing him with her mournful brown eyes. "Are you gonna be my friend?"

"Of course."

"Okay."

"On behalf of the Bank of America—good luck to you, Carmel."

She held his gaze a moment longer. "Everything's gonna be just everything." Adjusting the coat of the tweed suit over her narrow hips, she started up the front walk, straight and solemn and proud as an Indian princess; shaking a little on the inside.

He got her call at eight-thirty that night, having waited with exasperation and an odd kind of excitement since five.

"Hey, Jules. I got the job."

"Great. I'm glad. But I have to offset that with some news about your jalopy. You blew a piston out of the engine block, which is worse than it sounds. The man said it's not worth fixing."

"Life's dealt another cruel blow," Carmel said after a moment.

"But we have to celebrate your getting the job," he said, wondering at the advisability of pub-crawling in a strange town with a dusky Madonna.

"I's kinda done in, Jules, I put in a part day's work already."

"Perhaps I could come over there."

"Mmmhh, I can't do nothin' . . ." Her voice trailed off.

He feigned an audio difficulty, jiggling the receiver button. "What?"

"Yeah, I'm here. Okay, you come over for a while but I gotta turn in early."

"What's the address?"

"The Havila Apartments on Pacific. Nine hundred somethin'. I'm number—lessee—three-B."

"Crazy."

He had to execute a Gallagher and Shean shuffle on the narrow stairway, meeting a broad-beamed colored woman coming down with a pail of garbage, then up a second flight to 3-B, knocking gingerly.

In tight jeans and a violet sweater she opened the door a quarter of the way, riveting him with those somber eyes.

"Are you gonna be my friend?"

"I already said so."

"Okay." She stepped aside and let him in. "I ain't had time to get any furniture."

There was a mattress covered with bedding on the floor, a stove, refrigerator and the portable TV from the Morpheus Ranch Cottages which Julius had given her. The walls of the two rooms appeared to be of cardboard.

"All I got is some wine," Carmel said.

"Great."

From the cabinet over the sink she took down a bottle labeled California Sunburst Aperitif Wine, and Jules immediately kicked himself for not having brought something.

"On second thought maybe I'll settle for a Coke—or milk. Anything."

"I got Calso and some ice cream—Kona coffee."

"Ice cream. Crazy."

She filled two bowls with generous helpings and turned on the TV. They sat on the mattress watching a Susan Hayward movie. After a time she filled his bowl again and sat down watching him out of the corner of her eye.

"Wow, you're really stuffin' your face. I never seen anyone scarf cream like that."

"It's a weakness," Jules admitted.

"All sweets or just cream?"

"Cream."

"I gave you the last."

"I'm finished."

"I seen the movie before."

"It's not too great. . . . What are you writing?"

"A poem."

"Let me see."

She scribbled a few more lines, then handed him the album. He read carefully, rubbing a knuckle around his forehead.

> *Shelterd in the moony dead of night*
> *Waiting by lighted doves wings*
> *Dreams of jewls*
> *The man comes in patern spangeld*
> *Sweat cool and stickying*
> *Coming for Morpheus.*

Frowning with concentration, he read the lines again.

"Don't make fun of my endeavors," Carmel said.

"I'm not making fun. I just don't think I understand it."

"Never mind." She took the album back.

"Explain it to me. I've got an open mind. Something to do with sleep, dreams . . ."

"Just never mind." With an injured air, though you could tell nothing from her expression, she got up and switched channels on the TV. An informal talk-entertainment show came on. After ten minutes of the former, a girl in a cocktail dress sitting next to the moderator rose and walked in front of a screen backdrop. An invisible combo struck up an intro and the girl began singing, "It's the wrong time, and the wrong place . . ." legs slightly apart, shoulders moving, fingers snapping smartly on two and four. Carmel watched from a cross-legged position, body hunched forward, the knuckles of her right hand in her mouth.

"You look like you wish you were her," Jules said.

"That's a fact," Carmel said through her knuckles.

When the news came on at eleven she got up and turned off the set. "I got to be gettin' to bed. *Aaaaa-hnnn* . . ."

Jules stared at her. "What is it?"

"My jalopy. How'm I gonna get to work? I don't know the bus schedule."

"God, you gave me a jolt." He added after a moment, "I'll drive you."

"I got to be there at seven-thirty."

"Then I'll stay over," Jules said calmly.

For all of ten seconds she fixed him with that doleful gaze. "You said you were gonna be my friend."

"Jesus, all I'm suggesting is that I stay over and drive you to work. I think that's pretty friendly."

Carmel kept silently looking at him until a delicate knocking on the door made them both jump.

"Now who the devil—this hour o' night. Can't leave a body in peace . . ." she said with a slurred inflection, crossing to open the door.

A small, well-dressed, very dark Negro with a shining cherubic face stood on the threshold; the top of his rakish Tyrolean hat came about level with Carmel's eyes.

"Hello, I'm Henry. Neighbor of yours. I saw the light shining under your door and thought I might not be disturbing you."

"That's okay," Carmel said.

"I lives over you, sort of on the diagonal. Four-C."

"Uh-huh," Carmel said. "I was just gettin' ready for bed."

The Negro's gaze flicked past her shoulder, lighting briefly on Jules; smiling, he bobbed his head twice by way of greeting. "Since you just moved in I thought I'd tell you about some tires I have that I've been dispensing to my friends in the building at a very nominal fee, all brand-new and non-retread, come from my brother's tire and battery shop in San Bruno. Sort of surplus stock, you see, which he's forced to relinquish at consid'able loss . . ."

"I don't have a car no more. It fritzed out this mornin'."

Again the Negro's gaze flicked past her. "Perhaps your friend . . ."

"Sorry, I can't use any," Jules said. "Mine are practically new."

"Well you never knows when a tire's going to go on you. If you or any of your acquaintances find yourself in need I'm right upstairs, four-C. Henry's the name."

"Okay," Carmel said.

"And sorry to disturb you at this late hour." Smiling, he stepped back and bobbed his head, raising the Tyrolean hat a fraction.

"That's okay, Henry," Carmel said, closing the door. "That sound like the black market," she said to Jules, "and ah do mean black. Them boots is always out for a fast dollar."

"Boots?"

"It's an expression. Us."

"Really? And what are we? Me."

"Mmm, sometimes one thing, sometimes another. Paddies."

"Paddies! What's the derivation?"

"Huh?"

Jules shook his head. "We were talking about my staying over and driving you to work. It makes sense, no hassle, but if you'd prefer I left . . ."

Carmel studied him, soberly reflecting. "Outside the covers."

"Natch."

"Okay."

She went into the bathroom and Jules, exultant, actually trembling (Jesus, it's been such a long time, he told himself), straightened the bedding, neatly turning back the covers a quarter of the way on one side. He stood up, paced for a few minutes, then went to the door and applied the chain fastener, pulling the door open against it a few times to check its efficiency; finally he closed the door and flicked the lock button up, giving the door a few final test rattles.

Hearing the commotion, Carmel poked her head out of the bathroom. "What the devil you doin'?"

"Just locking up."

"You don't have to bolt us in, man, it's an in-tee-grated development," she said, reading his thoughts.

"I've yet to see any of us."

"They's one or two around."

A few minutes later she came out of the bathroom in a pale-blue cotton robe and got under the covers.

"Turn off the lights, Jules."

He did, then removed his shoes and lay down gingerly beside her.

Carmel gave a long-drawn-out sigh like a fat lady in distress, turned her back to him and fell, for all intents and purposes, into a deep sleep.

". . . keep on keepin' on," he thought he heard her murmur.

He lay there for almost a quarter hour, listening to distant sounds of doors opening and closing, toilets flushing, imperious garbled TV voices, then very lightly, tentatively, he reached under the covers and touched the small of her back.

"Go t' sleep, Chicken Little, we're gonna be friends," she said clearly.

"Crazy."

Goddam, shot down again. I don't believe it. Only twice since Gloria. Sic transit. *Your good fortune may never befall me, Cora Wasserman.* God bless . . . Muttering to himself, he shut his eyes tight and a while later surreptitiously eased under the top of the three blankets.

The alarm clock went off at six-thirty. He came awake with a jolt, eyes wide and staring at nothing, for a fraction of a moment hearing the morning school bell— that jangling gong of doom, brazen and irrevocable. Carmel reached out, pushed in the button and said distinctly, "I told a story. It's not a secre*tarial* position, it's house cleaning."

From under heavy lids he watched her cross the room, furl a page of newspaper and light the end with a match.

"Good God, what are you doing?"

"Gettin' the heat on." She turned the broiler jet, inserted the now flaming torch and presently the oven ignited with a hefty popping sound. She raced to the sink and got the flaring newspaper under a faucet.

"Why don't you use the heater?"

"Ah don't like the looks of it. Jules, I'm sorry, I got no coffee, nothin'."

"It doesn't matter," he said. "You look marvelous in pale blue."

"Yeah, they's quite a contrast in colors. . . . Man, I had me a dream. A weirdy."

"It's six-thirty in the morning and you're beautiful, Carmel."

"You dodo." She disappeared into the bathroom.

He drove her to the ivy-covered house on Jackson Street.

"What time will you be through?"

"Aroun' five, I guess."

"I'll pick you up."

"You really want to do that?"

"I'm your friend, aren't I?"

"Okay."

She got out of the car, an old trench coat covering the sweater and jeans, her hair in a yellow bandanna. Sticking her head in the driver's window a half foot from his face, she abruptly pushed her lips into Ubangi shape and intoned in a meandering down-home basso, "G'bye now, Jules. Y'all be good, heah?" Hattie McDaniel Brown.

Two blocks from his apartment Jules got a flat. He drove slowly, painfully to a station three blocks farther on, the car hobbling like a heavy man with a short leg. The mechanic on duty jacked it up. "You really want me to fix this?"

"Why not?"

"It's been repaired four times and the tread's gone."

Jules came around to look. "That's impossible, the car's practically new. It—" And he remembered Henry's dapper clothes, the shining cherubic face: "You never knows when a tire's going to go on you."

Eight

"Mr. Roman, I'm afraid your check for this month's rent was incorrect." She was holding the envelope he'd slipped under her door yesterday afternoon.

"Eighty dollars? I was sure I made it out for that."

"You're forgetting the auxiliary bill which I left with you."

"Seven seventy-five for a wet bathroom rug I thought was a bit exorbitant."

"There was a detailed listing of subsidiary damages in your bill."

Silently they regarded each other; behind the gold-rimmed spectacles she had Irene Bunning's cool molybdenum gaze. Jules' glance fell to the key ring, then rose again.

"I think I may be moving shortly, Mrs. Williams."

"That's your choice to make, Mr. Roman. Naturally I'll expect a final accounting before you do so. And I require one week's notice."

He started past her, up the stairs.

"Oh, and Mr. Roman . . ."

He stopped still, not turning.

"When you're away for several nights in succession, would you please see that your lights are all turned off?"

Mute, he continued up the stairs.

He saw now how she did it—why the rents were so reasonable, all utilities paid. She gouged it out of you in other ways. The fellow down the hall in 304 had been billed for painting his apartment; she had told him it was a shoddy job and that she'd have to have it done over by a professional. And when a tenant left—two had moved out last week—the vacancy was filled almost immediately. The turnover must be gratifying. . . . If only it weren't so damn comfortable here. The building was clean and quiet—a deceptive climate; from his kitchen alcove window there was a view of the bay and Nob and Telegraph hills which in another part of town he would have had to pay dearly for. And he'd recently bought some thrift-shop furniture—a lamp, bookstand, a solid round dining table and two chairs. The thought of moving, of starting over again with the want ads and phone calls, driving all over the city following up leads, then packing and hiring a van for the furniture, depressed him. But that might be decided for him if he refused to pay the auxiliary bill. Suddenly he remembered the thirty-five-dollar deposit he'd paid on top of the first month's rent. When he left it would be refunded, she had explained, minus a nominal vacancy cleaning charge and compensation for any breakage or damage. There was her lever, her ace in the hole; she got you coming and going. There'll come a day though, Mrs. Williams, when you'll get yours. . . .

He put on water for coffee, thinking about the past several nights. Carmel was scarcely to be believed: a lithe Black Beauty weighing in at one hundred eight

pounds sans libido, just managing to keep on keepin'
on, with visions of middle-class (secretarial) or artistic
(poetess, chanteuse) grandeur. And that barren cardboard pad—empty refrigerator, mattress on the floor.
The really incredible thing was, he hadn't made it yet!
No one could be expected to believe that—not the gang
at the U. of Conn., certainly not the leviathan colored
woman and her gloomy old man living beneath them,
one or the other of whom he saw at least once a day on
the stairway or through their open door. Carmel's am-
bivalence about her race was weird. When he'd told her
about the switched tire and his suspicions of Henry,
she'd said, tightening her mouth and bobbing her head,
"Yeah, well some o' them boots'll do anything for a
buck." There would have to be a confrontation with
Henry soon; he wouldn't let himself be intimidated. Of
course there was the slim chance that Henry might not
have been responsible. The switch could have taken
place days before while he was parked during an interview—he'd been in some pretty grim neighborhoods—
and he simply hadn't noticed it until the tire went flat.
What he'd do, he'd bide his time, feel Henry out, make
sure. There might be a way of setting a trap, chalking all
four tires, unobtrusively, and only at night when he was
parked in the Havila lot. Two days ago he'd told Mergy
what had happened (omitting his own suspicions) and
the voucher for a new tire had gone through, but—and
this was the kicker—Mergy had asked him point blank
if he'd been parked in "Darky-town"!

Crazy.

It had been a rough month; a hard day's night. There

were times when he almost wished he was back at Weaver Street School. Almost. At least there the harassment had come from only one direction, life was a good deal simpler, more consistent. The continual tumult from the rows of desks, Bunning stealing into his room like a thief in rubber-soled brogues (how the woman had been able to open that door so soundlessly was something he'd never comprehend); the Nile River regularly overflowed its banks . . .

Midafternoon he drove to North Beach to meet Carmel at Dante's Excelsior Coffeehouse. She was occupying her customary Saturday-afternoon table in the window alcove, the autograph album open before her.

"Hey, Jules. Look what came this mornin'."

From the wicker bag she took out a folded typewritten page to which was clipped a printed slip from *Mademoiselle: . . . number of manuscripts prevents us from making individual comment . . . regret we cannot at this time make an offer of publication.*

"See, they was *int*'rested. Maybe if I added a couple lines and sent it back . . ."

He hadn't the heart to tell her it was a form rejection slip. He read the poem, erratically typed on a public-library machine, and found, besides the expected unintelligibility, a half dozen misspelled words. "Why don't you use a dictionary?" he said, pointing out the errors.

Carmel frowned; a furtive, scattered look crept into the mournful brown eyes. "I tried to look 'em all up."

He slowly let out his breath. It was true—if you didn't know that "curtins" was spelled with an "a" and "wisper" with an "h," then neither Webster's Third International nor the Oxford Collegiate was going to tell you. "Next time you send something out let me see it first."

"Okay." She lightly patted his thigh. "You're a good friend, Jules."

"Who's the bearded guy staring at us?"

"That's O'Hara. He's the first person I met here. He got me my place at Havila."

"He looks like Van Gogh."

"Naw, it's O'Hara."

They ordered espresso from the waitress.

"I may have to move pretty soon," Jules said.

"There's a vacancy at Havila. Four-E."

"That would be down the hall from Henry."

"Yeah," Carmel said, bobbing her head.

"I didn't come cross-country to move down the hall from Henry. I mean it was a long trip and I don't require Henry as a neighbor, if you know what I mean."

"Yeah, I knows what you mean." She patted his thigh again.

"Have you noticed the salty looks we've been getting mornings from that couple downstairs?"

"That's Reba Mae and Elmer. They's good folk, Jules. You're imaginin' things."

"Maybe, maybe. . . . Jesus, there are some weird-looking people in here."

"Yeah, mostly all paddies you'll notice."

"Here comes your friend Van Gogh."

"Uh-huh."

O'Hara turned a chair around, straddled it, and ignoring Jules, said, "How you getting along at Havila?"

"Okay. This is my friend Jules. He's lookin' for a place too."

The man turned to him, light-blue eyes glinting; his skin was pale but curiously blotched, and Jules wondered, with a twinge of revulsion, what manner of life the coarse, wiry, reddish beard might conceal. "Would you care to change your luck?"

"What do you mean?"

"There's a small apartment-hotel near here occupied almost exclusively by Chinese hookers. A room plus kitchenette on the ground floor is vacant. Very reasonable, and needless to say, lots of good company."

The pale eyes glittered, but Jules couldn't tell whether the mouth was smiling.

"That's not quite what I had in mind."

"Just a thought." He turned back to Carmel. "There's a chap sounds like it could be your brother working at JC's Bar-B-Q on Steiner Street."

"You mean it? Where's that at?"

"The Fillmore. San Francisco's Harlem, so to speak."

"Jules, c'n we go down there this afternoon?"

"I don't think I can today. I have some reports to make out."

"Ha!" O'Hara slapped the table, emitting a low, guttural chuckling sound. Jules met his eyes; he had the disquieting feeling that he was being put on. There was a bright stony arrogance in the man's gaze.

"Got to take care of business." O'Hara rose now, straddle-legged, his callused paint-stained hands gripping the back of the chair; he stared briefly at Jules. "Arrivederch." He twisted the chair about, planted it firmly under the table and strode out the door.

"I can't say I'm particularly taken with your friend. I wouldn't say he's exactly my kind of folk, as the saying goes."

"He's been a help, Jules. He got me the apartment an—"

"I wouldn't trust him from here to Grant Avenue."

"We's on Grant, Jules."

"Precisely."

"Ooeee, you jiggy today. You don't like nobody or *nothin'*."

"I'd be a bit less jiggy if you'd succumb."

"Huh?"

"*Give in.* Jesus, surely you understand what I'm talking about."

"You be a good boy now or I'll bite your face." She patted his thigh again. He propped his elbows on the table and bent his face in his hands, gazing dully at the sheet of poetry through splayed fingers.

Curtins of night bellow in darkness

"Come on now, Jules, you gettin' all irritable. Are you comin' to JC's Bar-B-Q with me?"

"Next September." The frustration was almost too much to bear.

"Go ahead, you just keep on like that. . . . Well, I'm goin' on down there. You be a good boy while I's gone, heah? Mammy don't want you gettin' yourself in any mischief in the in-tee-rim, *nohow*. You listenin' to me, Jules?"

Nine

"I can't hack it this mornin', I ain't gonna be able to face the nation." Carmel flung her arm over and poked the alarm button. "I'm gettin' ready to call an' tell another story, Jules."

He turned over and got his head under the pillow, constantly astonished at how she was able to come instantly awake out of an ostensibly deep sleep, speaking distinctly and rationally. In a week and a half he had graduated to a position under the top two covers, sans pants and shirt; but that was as far as he was getting.

"How's this sound?" Her voice took on a precise Caucasian inflection: "Mrs. Cameron? This is Carmel. . . . Not too well, thank you. I'm afraid I've come down overnight with some variety of bug. Yes, possibly the *int*estinal flu. . . . Uh-huh, there does seem to be a lot of it going around, yes'm. I may feel somewhat better this afternoon but I really can't promise . . ." And in the fluting tones of Mrs. Cameron: " 'You poor deah, what a shame. Is there anything I can bring you? Some hot chicken broth perhaps . . .' You is a jewel, Mizcameron, some South'n-frahd chicken broth, yes'm. Mmmmm-*mmh*." She sprang up, as always in the blue cotton robe, and drew a page of newspaper from the pile under the sink.

Jules came out from under the pillow, watching the insane procedure, the *blammmm* of gas igniting, her dash to the sink, getting the torch under the faucet just as it began really flaring, blazing down toward her hand. He had shown her how to light the gas heater, made her do it a couple of times under supervision, but the next morning she'd gone back to the broiler. "Oven heat's better, Jules," she told him. "When we was a family up north I'd come downstairs mornin's and my old man'd always have that big stove blazin' full blast."

Now he watched her lift the receiver, biting her lip as she painstakingly dialed the number. "Mrs. Cameron? Uh—this is Carmel . . ." Watched, fascinated, as she told her story in an admirably controlled tone, the narrow face taut, showing the strain. ". . . possibly some kind of bug, I believe . . ." hand coming down flat on her head, pop-eyed, half play-acting for his benefit, now slumping against the wall, sliding excruciatingly down the length of it as she got into the real meat of the fabrication, then pausing, listening with mock anguish, dismay, self-pity, a wealth of fleeting theatrical emotions crossing the stark brown face, and suddenly smiling, her face lighting up in a round-chinned elfin grimace of delight. "Yes, I will, Mrs. Cameron, thank you . . . Yeah. Goodbye." Virtually sprawled on the floor, she hung up in triumph.

"That's the second time this week," Jules said. "You can fool the upper classes only some of the time, baby."

"Well ah didn't come all the way from St. Helena to be no do*mes*tic. I's gonna spend the mornin' writin' and this P.M. go out 'n' get me a singin' job."

"Crazy. Good luck. On behalf of the Bank of America."

Abruptly her face resumed its grave and melancholy cast. She crossed the room and sank to her knees in the blue robe beside Jules, her face scant inches from his. "Is you Mammy's baby? Is you?" She began covering his face with birdlike kisses. "Did baby bunting have a good sleep? Did-he-have-a-good-*sleep?*" Kiss, kiss, kiss, kiss. "Mammy's baby wants to grow up to be a big boy, doesn't he. Doesn't he? Hmmm?" Cradling his head in her arms, rocking to and fro, then shaking him by the shoulders, pecking again at his eyes and nose and chin.

"You're insane!" Jules cried, breaking up.

"A big *boy.*"

"Crazy boot . . ." Still laughing, he got his hands on her hard little breasts. She sprang off him like a cat.

"You behave yourself, Chicken Little."

"You really are a little out of your mind, do you know that?"

"I'm gonna bite your face."

"Unbelievable."

She went into the kitchen and came back with two glasses of grapefruit juice. Arms extended, perfectly balanced, she sank gracefully, slowly, as if lowered by puppet strings, to a cross-legged position on the mattress and handed him one of the glasses. "I never spilled a drop yet."

"It's one of your better bits."

"I dreamt about Longwell again last night an'—this is queer, Jules—I dreamt I was dreamin' about him."

"Say that again."

"I dreamt I was dreamin' about him."

"Okay."

"And—I dunno whether to tell you this—he had nothing."

"What?"

"He didn't have a thing. You know, where he's supposed to have it."

"Jesus. And I thought I had problems."

"Will you go to the Fillmore with me tonight? I wanna look around again. I don't like walkin' there alone." She'd gone to JC's Bar-B-Q on Saturday, but the new chap working there was shorter and heavier than her brother; not like Longwell at all.

"Why not? They're your people."

"Yeah, I know why you didn't wanna come with me."

"Why? Enlighten me."

She gave him a sober, wary look. "Like the rest o' the paddies, you're afraid o' your skin."

Jules shook his head briefly, a dog coming out of water. "I'm not afraid. I just think your chances of finding him aren't worth the effort. I'm sure O'Hara was putting you on Saturday."

"Now why would he do that?"

"I'm not sure—partly to get to me. There's something sinister about that bastard . . ."

"He's your people, Jules," Carmel said, almost smiling.

"Not under the skin he isn't." His hand, resting on her shin, eased surreptitiously under the blue robe. She bent double from the waist and bit hard.

"Dumb boot!"

"Paddy!"

"This is brutal! It's not fair to sleep with someone and not sleep with them!"

"I just can't *do* nothin' now, Jules. Maybe someday."

"That may be too late."

"What you mean?"

Wordlessly he shook his head.

"There you go cuttin' yourself off, shakin' that head." She gazed languorously at him, the whites of her eyes moony, opaline. "Are you comin' with me to the Fillmore tonight?"

"All right. Yes." He'd get it over with: establish his courage, simultaneously free himself of O'Hara's intimidation. And hopefully that would be the end of looking for Longwell, the vanishing boot. "I'll go—just this once. Even if it means getting my throat slit."

"You dodo, you're so fearful. I'm gonna bite your face." And she did, taking one whole side of it between her strong teeth like a tigress gripping her cub, his jawbone clamped in an ivory vise.

He started to break up again. "You maniac!" he cried through clenched teeth, this time getting his hand under the robe good. The gorgeous sensation shot up his arm, culminating painfully in his face where Carmel's teeth were clamping down in earnest.

He wrenched away feeling his cheek and jaw for blood.

"Dumb black bitch!"

"Whitey! Shithead!" She bounced up and made for the bathroom, her sanctum sanctorum, poking her head back out the door for a second, baring her strong horse teeth and shaking her delicate fist at him, an exacerbated Brown Bomber.

Ten minutes later he followed her into the bathroom and virtually slit his throat while washing his face.

"*Carmel!*"

She opened the door and stuck her head in. "Miss Brown to . . . Lawd, yo' *bloody.*"

"*What's your razor blade doing in the soap?*"

"Ohhh. Ah'm sorry. . . . What a dodo." Her face crumpled like a child's, taking on a scattered life-is-too-much-for-me look.

"But what's it doing embedded in the *soap?*"

"Here, lemme fix it." She soaked a face cloth in cold water and gingerly applied it to the gash.

"Jesus, you're a . . . mass of contradictions! A veritable mass!" he cried, half breaking up at the sound of his own voice, but angry, exasperated, grinning crookedly in spite of himself even as he saw in the mirror the face cloth darkening with his own blood; and higher up, the still visible teeth marks laid into jaw and cheekbone. "This is insane! What in Christ's name am I doing in this . . . integrated barracks?"

"I dunno, Jules, I just don't know. No suh. Ooeee, you really bleedin' . . ."

"Get me a Band-Aid. A big one."

"Jules, I don't have none."

"I don't believe it."

"Ah'm sorry . . ."

"You've got nothing in this godforsaken place! Civilized people sleep in beds with legs, they sit on chairs, eat—"

"You know I'm savin' for another car."

"Baby, don't get one. You're a menace."

"I don't like you talkin' to me like that . . ." Rubbing a tiny fist in her eye, the thin brown face crumpling again, desolate against the blue robe.

"For Christ's sake. All right. Just get me another cloth—a clean one."

"I's gettin' it, Jules."

Holding the cloth to his throat, he let her help him into his coat.

"We don't have to go to the Fillmore tonight if you don't want."

"Good. I wouldn't care to get my throat slit twice in twenty-four hours." Her face started to come apart again. "All right, Jesus, no tears. Please; I retract it. I'm in a shitty mood. I've got eight hours ahead of me that I don't care to think about."

"You got to keep on keepin' on, Jules."

"Yeah." At the door he pressed his cheek to hers. "Good night, Irene."

"It's mornin', Jules."

"I know."

He went down the stairway, and of course Reba Mae, right on schedule, opened her door, stooping with a pneumatic sigh to collect the milk and newspaper. She glanced up at him with hooded eyes, nodding her head slightly (*What's that crazy paddy doin' with a wash cloth 'round his neck?*), then looking behind him, wondering where Carmel was. Out of the corner of his eye he saw her husband Elmer through the open doorway, sitting heavily at the enameled kitchen table in shorts and undershirt, gazing glumly out at him. Easing past Reba Mae, he heard a heavy clunking sound as of something dropping to the floor.

"What's the problem in there?" Reba Mae said, straightening up with an effort.

"There's no problem, woman," Elmer answered dourly. "Why should there be a problem?"

Jesus, what *am* I doing here? he asked himself again, continuing down the stairs. It made no sense at all. Sitting cross-legged on a mattress every night like a bloody Indian in the middle of a practically barren pad with cardboard walls in a veritable barracks building (integrated? not from where he was sitting), the only human touch the hand-sewn polka-dot curtains that hung lopsided over the kitchen window, watching hoary movies and "Hullabaloo" while Miss Brown sang-along and frugged, scarfin' the cream, *yassuh*, then going to bed and not even *getting* any. He should be going out nights, meeting people, decent white folk, *yeah*, dating girls of his own social milieu. Uh-*huh*. Her nonsexuality was really astounding, contrary to everything he'd been led to believe about the race (an asinine generality, all right, but—); there must have been some kind of hang-up in her past life.

In the parking lot he inspected the chalk marks on his tires: everything was in order. If Henry had been abroad last night, he'd hit on someone else's wheels. (Or had he discovered the ruse?) Jesus, he must be truly insane to subject himself to this kind of pressure. What for? Maybe he ought to make a clean break, sever relations. Why go through all this anguish with people like Henry and Reba Mae and Elmer (wondering why Carmel was messin' 'round with that white New England trash; no one in his right mind would believe they weren't making it) and that sinister son of a bitch

O'Hara baiting him into a trip to the Fillmore. What
did he need that for? He could get comparable treatment every day on the job. One of these nights he was
going to get his throat slit for real. Welcome to California indeed. Horsback never saw this kind of action; he
didn't know what he was talking about. . . . Jules suddenly grinned, imagining his father's reaction to Carmel, admittedly an improbable confrontation: "Dad,
meet my girl friend, Carmel Brown." Old Cosine
Squared would give her the slow once-over, then turn to
him with that glazed rueful look of dismay. "Goddam,
what goes with you guys, anyway?" Not that his father
was a bigot, but he did have somewhat set ideas about
class consciousness and responsibility to one's self, the
importance of keeping the line of one's life clear and
untrammeled: straight ahead. Of course, Earl was not
precisely his own best example. The truth was, this
wasn't at all the new life he had imagined; he wasn't
enjoying the city and he was lonely as hell. And despite
Carmel's infantile fantasies, her virtually total inability
to cope with day-to-day life, the cunning lies and pitiful
aspirations, there was something undeniably congenial
about her, a degree of kindredness between them; that
and the supple chocolate body which he'd better pos-
sess soon if he was to maintain his sanity. They were
attuned, there was no question of it, in an odd way they
sustained each other, both anxious, undirected, a little
afraid (he admitted it), hating their jobs, neither with a
tangible alternative. . . . With a pang of uneasiness he
thought of his final interview yesterday. He'd gained
admittance to the house all right—no Indian tribe in a
teepee or brood of Mexicans in a brush hut here but a

solid average middle-class residence in the Sunset District (he was becoming increasingly sensitive to social strata or Subjective Economic Ratings, as the instruction sheet phrased it)—and was three pages into the first magazine when the woman excused herself to check something in the kitchen. Her kid, sitting on the floor with crayons and a coloring book, mean-looking, with the locked wizened face of an old man, had stared sullenly at him, periodically sticking out his tongue like a viper, until he'd said quietly, meaning only to *think* it, "Don't stick your tongue out at me, baby, I'm not your old man." Of course the mother had chosen that precise moment to return from the kitchen; she had stopped stock-still, mouth open, blinking like an automaton, then had curtly asked him to leave. He'd gathered up the magazines and, disbelieving his own ears, had heard himself say on the way out, "That kid of yours could use a good swift kick in the can."

Bloody job was beginning to get to him.

His heart gave a leap as he turned into Potrero and saw the navy-blue Volks parked down the street—but now with a black and yellow Cal license plate. Was it the same car? He was tempted to wait until the blonde came out of whichever house she was in—if it was the blonde. Maybe she too was lonely for a back-East contact. Forty or no, he wouldn't mind a taste of something from old Tolland County. . . . But he couldn't very well confront her with a blood-soaked wash cloth. Depressed, he went inside, past Mrs. Williams' closed forbidding door and upstairs to properly shave and apply a Band-Aid to his slit throat.

At five o'clock, after a miserable day, he drove back to

the barracks. Carmel wasn't home. He let himself in and fidgeted for an hour or so, watching TV, listening to part of a Billie Holiday LP; he finished off the rest of the open carton of Kona coffee while glancing through a slim library booklet entitled *Dreams: the Language of the Subconscious*. Her brother without a thing where he's supposed to have it, he remembered. Freud and Jung, *et al.*, would have a field day with that one. Toward seven he put a TV dinner in the oven, lighting the broiler in the normal non-torch way and singeing all the hair off the back of his hand.

Shortly after eight o'clock he drove to Dante's, expecting to find her socked in at the window table scribbling her unintelligible odes to the unconscious. That was really something. Miss Edna St. Vincent Brown. The day she had a poem published he'd be chosen Northern California's Teacher of the Year. But hope beats eternal: He wished he had a semblance of her faith, misguided as it was. Last week she told him she had met a man who was going to publish a book of her poems. When he interrogated her and the fabrication finally came out (the man was a student she'd met at Dante's who had told her he'd like to see more of her poems because he had a friend who knew a publisher in Berkeley) she had looked almost surprised. Her inventions were becoming more guileful, less conscious.

The coffeehouse waitress said she had been in during the afternoon and left around four. As he turned to go he thought he recognized O'Hara in the gloomy recesses of the place, those glittering stone-blue eyes fixed silently on him.

He went to a movie and drove back to the barracks,

freshly chalking all four tires before going upstairs. The apartment was empty. He started to open the fresh half gallon of ice cream, caught himself, undressed, and after an hour of listening to the distant barracks noises, trying to differentiate between live and TV voices, drifted into a fitful sleep.

Sometime after two he opened his eyes—momentarily disoriented—saw two apparently disembodied white orbs floating over him, peering down, and came bolt upright, stifling a scream. With a little gasping sound Carmel backed in terror against the wall, setting the clothes hangers on the pole jangling musically.

"Jesus, you scared me."

"I scared *you*? Lawdy." She steadied the hangers. "Why'd you scream?"

"I didn't scream."

"It sounded kinda close to one."

"Where have you been?"

"Listen, Jules, get ready for some news. I got me a job singing."

"Where?" he said curtly.

"Well, a little place on Broadway."

"When do you start?"

"Uh, Friday night, I think, if—"

"What does it pay?"

"I don't know yet. You see, the man—"

"Goddam," he said, angry, "what are you lying for? Have you got a job or haven't you?"

Across the dark room the milk-white orbs regarded him silently, reproachfully. "Well, it's more like a afternoon au*dition*. But the man told me if he liked me I could maybe start that same night. Friday."

"Okay. What do you have to keep on *lying* for?" He got up, strode to the door in his jockey shorts and set the chain fastener in position.

"There you go boltin' us in again. Why're you so fearful?"

"Because I'm too goddam young to get my throat slit is why." He switched on the overhead light, opened the refrigerator and tore the flap off the ice cream.

Carmel soberly watched him spoon it into a big bowl. "I don't know how come you don't put on any weight always stuffin' your face, scarfin' up that Kona coffee."

Ten

He set out to enjoy the nighttime city. He had phoned her at Mrs. Cameron's and told her he wouldn't be able to pick her up today; he seriously meant not to call her or see her again—at least not at the barracks, not on the old basis. There was just too much anguish, not enough compensation. If she phoned, he'd tell her just that, couched in comprehensible terms. They would remain friends, of course, they would always be attuned (in a secret unfledged corner of his heart he'd always be Mammy's baby!), but he had to start stretching out and making other contacts if San Francisco was to become home.

So he started with a solitary drink in the Crown Room atop the Fairmont Hotel's Tower where the uniformly tall waitresses wore slit brocaded gowns and powdered periwigs, gazing down through a mammoth picture window at the glittering city and reflecting on his generally inauspicious start in the Golden State and dismal future as a consumer research field representative (talk about euphemisms!). Yesterday the mother of the viper-tongued brat had phoned in and finked on him. He'd tried to explain his side of the story, but Mergy had interrupted him: "Kiddo, whatever the provocation, when we start antagonizing prospective respondents we're in trouble. I mean what is the point of cutting our own throats?" Jesus, the futility, the sheer senselessness: tying his stomach in a knot trying to explain to the likes of Mergy why he'd been unable to complete the showing of a back issue of *Redbook* with Debbie Reynolds in a Santa Claus suit on the cover.

"Another Scotch, sir."

"I guess not. Not much happening here."

"A bit quiet on week nights."

"You can say that again."

The bartender declined, moving down the bar, working diligently on the gleaming surface with a towel.

He took the outside glass-walled elevator down, packed into the hermetic chamber with two dozen bug-eyed tourists slowly dropping twenty-three stories through the jeweled firmament, and re-entered the sultry October night—San Francisco's brief displaced summer: like August in Willimouth.

North Beach, then, was the place to go, he knew, but away from Dante's; circumventing Dante's. Parking in the Beach would be impossible on such a night. He boarded a cable car at the crest of California Street and, hanging on an outside pole, swinging loosely out over the street—on the sidewalk a boy and a plump lady in violet stretch pants trained their cameras on him—rode it down to line's end: the financial district where the sheer jutting buildings made canyons of the streets, a bit of Manhattan in old San Francisco. From there a six-block walk to the Beach, the sidewalks aswarm with bright summer dresses and shirtsleeves, a soft slow dazed quality about the strollers as if they couldn't believe the unaccustomed weather; the cool gray fogbound town almost steaming—New York tenement weather, close, sweltering. Jules loosened his tie, took off his sport coat and slung it over his shoulder. Overhead, spanning Columbus Avenue, a banner proclaiming *Society DiMaria S. S. Del Lume* hung limply, and suddenly now a dark gleaming convertible commandeered by a deeply tanned red-haired queen roared under the banner as if trying to bust open the heat-locked town, the car's fenders and trunk emblazoned with large block letters in white paint: I AM A BONAFIDE LEMON . . . CHRYSLER'S GUARANTEE IS A PUT-ON . . . ALL CHRYSLER EXECS ARE FINKS. The throng of pedestrians sending up a rousing clamor which followed the big car down Broadway like a wake. Jules threaded his way through the crowd, trying to find walking and breathing space. Under a marquee announcing TOPLESS DANCERS—FRUG, TWIST, JERK a strange tandem had become the cynosure of attention: a prodigious male brute wearing a lacy pink dress and white ankle socks accompanied by a diminutive and elegant faggot in a white linen suit. "The weirdos are out tonight," the woman next to Jules said. The brute in drag was exchanging badinage with the crowd. Now he raised his arms heavenward displaying huge perspiration hoops and cried in a dulcet mincing voice, "It's positively Adriatic out tonight!" The brazen mascaraed eyes abruptly lowered; catching Jules' gaze and holding it for an excruciatingly long moment —transfixed, Jules found himself unable to tear his eyes away—he remarked languidly, "Well aren't you too fucking much."

"Crazy."

Jules ducked into the topless club, found a place at

the bar and drank two Scotches to a pandemonium of twanging guitars and crashing drums, watching with a kind of dull fever the ponderous bouncing breasts of the two girls on either side of the crimson-jacketed rock combo, while out front some fifty couples writhed and bobbed, arms cranking with mechanical abandon.

Two men standing behind him were passed their drinks over his head.

"I thought the broads in this town were supposed to fall all over you," one said.

"Let's hit on the two dancers when they get off. They can't keep their jugs going like that indefinitely."

"Are you kidding? There'll be a line of studs a block long."

Jules downed his drink and elbowed his way to the exit. Outside, the crowds had thickened; the air was clammy, motionless, the blazing street strident with horns from backed-up traffic. A murky starless sky hung heavy, tangible as a canopy. Long ways from Willimouth, Jules thought. He felt torpid, lead-limbed; his shirt was drenched with sweat. He stared dully at the cars in the traffic-choked street, his gaze lighting unbelievingly on a red Karmann Ghia with the blue and white license plate. Two young girls, long-haired, chic-looking. Unhesitatingly he stepped into the street and stooped to the open driver's window. "Hi, I'm from Willimouth. What town are you from?" The girl stared briefly at him, then with an almost imperceptible lift of the eyebrows calmly rolled up the window, turned to her friend and began an animated conversation.

With egg on his face, Jules required a moment or two to straighten up. "Fuck Mr. Roman," he murmured.

The prospect of retreat was humiliating. He threaded his way through the cars beginning to inch forward now —a blasting klaxon brought him up on his toes—and reached the other side. Through the open door of the Krazy Kat Saloon came plunking banjos and a booming chorus of voices: "We will be happy, Nellie, bye . . . and . . . bye . . ." He stepped inside. Two banjoists in candy-striped shirts and sleeve garters sat atop a frontless upright piano, their feet dangling in the pianist's face; alongside them on the small stage a paunchy, wildly bearded bald man in a plaid flannel shirt and Levis ferociously plucked a gut-bucket, madly stomping his foot out of tempo. The room was stifling, packed to the walls with a college-age crowd, faces flushed, banging their schooners on the wooden tables and singing at the tops of their lungs. Jules managed to get a schooner of beer and leaned against the wall listening to the old beer-party tunes he used to sing at the U. of Conn., but numb, detached, unable to feel a part of it. His head began to throb in synchronization to the thumping gut-bucket.

During a lull between numbers he asked the boy next to him, "Are there any quieter places around?"

"Try the Nob Hill hotels."

"I've come from there. Too quiet."

"There's the King of Hearts around the corner. But this is the best entertainment in town." The boy turned to look at him. "Haven't I seen you around here before?"

"No. And you're not likely to again." Jules set his empty schooner on the edge of a table and started out.

"No accounting for taste," the boy called mildly after him.

At the King of Hearts a handful of people were sitting around the piano bar. It was darker and much cooler in here. He sat alone at the long alternate bar, his coat draped over his knees, and ordered a drink from the Negro bartender, staring at himself in the mirror over the row of bottles, listening to the piano-bass duo playing Gershwin—"A Foggy Day," then "Nice Work If You Can Get It." With the streets and other clubs jammed he wondered why business should be so poor in this cool and comfortable bar. Could it be that quiet tasteful music, unadorned and devoid of gimmicks, simply didn't make it any more? In this most cosmopolitan of cities? Difficult to believe. On his second Scotch a woman slipped onto the stool beside him. He studied her in the mirror: short, big-breasted, a bit on the dumpy side—but reasonably pretty, or once pretty; it was hard to tell in the dim light. Overhead the blades of a fan whirred softly.

"What are you so sad about, honey?"

"I'm not sad," Jules spoke to her mirror image. "Just reflecting. Getting loaded."

"Everyone's sad to you, Dori," the bartender said, working on the place in front of her with a rag.

The woman cocked her head at him. "Don't put me in the trick bag in front, Francis."

Jules didn't know what that meant but he liked the ring of it.

Dori was rummaging in her purse. "Buy me a drink, honey. I'm on the outs."

Jules put a dollar bill on the bar. Ride along with it, easy, no resistance; but his heart was beginning to bump against his ribs.

"You got girl trouble?" Dori looked genuinely solicitous. "I can't believe that. Nice-looking young guy like you. Good eyes. Hazel."

"Gray," Jules said. "Have you ever met anyone by the name of Horsback?" he asked, still speaking to the mirror.

Dori took a long swallow of her drink, watching him obliquely. "No, honey, but in my childhood there was a kid named Lester Newburger. We used to call him Lobster."

"Another Scotch," Jules said to the bartender, feeling suddenly good about Dori. "My girl looks like a princess —or a poetess. Lean and unbelievably supple. Like a willow. Great dark eyes." The Queen of Spades, he added tacitly and began to laugh, a bit out of control.

Dori rattled the ice cubes in her empty glass. "Don't describe beautiful chicks to me, honey. I get depressed."

The good pianist was into Jerome Kern. "Long Ago and Far Away."

"Let's get out of here," Dori said. "My place is comfy. Soft lights, records."

Jules turned now and took a long, somewhat drunken look at her. The face fleshy but clear-skinned, a full mouth, lips thickish; the eyes were deep-set and old. No Carmel Brown, that's for sure, nossuh; no Gloria Deitweiler. "I haven't much money left."

"It's only twenty, honey."

"I could manage but ten," he said rather thickly,

spacing the words.

"Oh, honey, that's an awful put-down. I have stand-ards to maintain. Fifteen and we'll do it up right."

The juices were pumping in his groin. His mind played a neat trick, reverting to Fat Harvey's used-car lot and the windshield placard PLENTY MILES IN THE OLD GAL: A GORGEOUS CHASSIS. No stopping now.

"Not your place," he said, conjuring up accomplices lurking in dark closets. "Mine," he said, thinking of Mrs. Williams, the more appealing of two dismal alter-natives.

"Whatever you say, honey." She was off the stool, purse in hand. "Leave Francis a nice tip."

Sighing, he dredged the change out of his pocket, sixty, seventy cents.

"Have a nice evening," Francis called pleasantly after them.

Outside, a cooling breeze had sprung up, over Broad-way's luminous blur three stars gleaming palely through dark-tinged shredded clouds.

"Goddam," Jules said.

"What, honey?"

"My car's on Nob Hill."

"We can take a cab there."

They waited five minutes. The crowds were thinning; "Moon River" floated faintly out from the King of Hearts. In the sharp-chilled air the edge of desire blunted. He draped his coat over one shoulder, rubbing an eye with the heel of his palm.

A cab pulled up. The driver reached back, expression-less, and opened the door.

"I suppose you won't believe this is the first time for

me," he said when they were under way. "I mean, for money . . ."

"Honey, I believe anything and everything." And she fell toward him, tongue furry-hot in his ear, hand like a vise on his crotch.

They got past Mrs. Williams' door without incident —Jules assuring himself, It wouldn't matter, she doesn't really look like a whore—and went upstairs.

"My place is cozier," Dori said, starting to undress. "Where's your john?"

Jules pointed wordlessly, gnawed by the disquieting feeling that he had left something important somewhere. When Dori emerged a few minutes later naked, he remembered: his sport coat in the taxi.

Dori did not have a gorgeous chassis.

"Come on, honey, get ready."

The phone rang.

"Don't answer it."

"I'm not."

It was over, undressing and all, in a matter of minutes. At the point of climax three words escaped his lips: Friend, Roman, countryman.

Jesus, he thought sadly, it's been such a long time.

Down the hall a radio was playing.

Dori was up and dressing.

"Stay," Jules said.

"It'll be thirty more for the night, honey."

Jules spread his hands wordlessly.

"Say toot," Dori said, jacknifed, fastening her bra.

She was standing beside the bed, fully dressed, waiting.

"Sorry." He got up, took a five and a ten from his wallet and handed them to her.

"I'll need cab fare, honey."

"I have three dollars left—to my name."

"I can't walk to the Beach from here, honey."

He handed the rest over. She tucked the bills not in her bra, as he had envisioned whores did, but in her purse. Plenty miles in the old gal yet.

"Stop by the place again. I'm there most every night."

Jules opened the door for her, hiding his nudity behind it.

"Bye, honey."

"Good night, Irene."

"Dori, silly."

"Good night, Dori. And my best to Lobster Newburger."

He closed the door, got the shower attachment down from the shelf in the bedroom closet. The phone was ringing. Into the tub, cramped sitting position, running the water steaming hot; with the hose clamped between his knees, sending the scalding needle spray tattooing against his chest, he soaped himself carefully, luxuriously. Steam rose in billows around him. *I think that's enough on that particular spot, Roman . . . Thank you very much . . .*

"Hello, it's me," he always used to say when Gloria answered the phone.

"Hello, me," she'd always say back.

Eleven

The phone woke him the next morning. It rang every few minutes, insistently, while he shaved and dressed. Willfully closing his mind to the King of Hearts and the Queen of Spades, he allowed it to ring away as he closed the door behind him. Throughout the day's interviews he tried to remember the company name of the cab in which he'd left his sport coat, and finally, at five o'clock, resorted to the expedient of calling every company in the yellow pages. No lost coat had been reported. "That figures, your driver was the same build as me," he said in exasperation to the last woman, and hung up. He immediately called back, said, "Listen, I just spoke to you. That was an uncalled-for remark and I apolo—" and heard the line click dead in his ear.

He had only change in his pockets, sixty-five cents, hardly enough for a meal and well short of the price of a movie ticket even at one of the fleabag houses. Pay day was two days away. At home was a tomato, a jar of pimento Cheez Whiz and the stale end of a loaf of sourdough. The office was closed and there was no place where he was well enough known to cash a check. My right arm to see Horsback cantering down the street right now: on behalf of the Bank of America . . . It's really astonishing that I can still smile, he told himself.

He found a parking place in North Beach and began walking aimlessly, past the previous night's clubs, helical neon tubing dead and dusty in the waning afternoon light. The temperature must have dropped twenty degrees since last night and he could smell the fog. The weather changes in this town were not to be believed. Back in Willimouth there'd be frost on the ground mornings, the smell of dying leaves and apples . . . He sniffed tentatively but couldn't remember.

He found himself a half block from Dante's; he hadn't meant to come this way. As obliquely as possible now he stole a glance at the window table: empty. Damn. In the gloomy recesses, shadowy figures were hunched over tables. He walked on.

"Hey."

A coarse arrogant call; surely not for him.

"Hey!"

He turned and saw O'Hara's lumber-jacketed figure in the doorway, the nineteenth-century bearded artisan's face stony with disdain.

"What?" Jules said.

"Not with your friend tonight?"

Jules waited, waited out the pale arrogant eyes.

"She was in last night with a chap. Soul brother."

Jules waited.

"You're not talking. I hear you changed your luck last night."

Jules shook his head, shaking off the water. "I'm not following you."

"I'm speaking of Dori, of course."

"You're well informed."

"She keeps me posted like a good ex-wife should."

Jules felt a twinge of disgust, his eyes dropping to the thick tangled blond beard. Any future inclination he might have had to look up Dori again was now definitely precluded.

"You oughtn't to be cheating, Friend. Have the courage of your convictions. If you're going to have a spade old lady go it the whole way, no mincing around. Simple, straightforward, uncomplicated. A black-and-white situation, so to speak."

Could O'Hara possibly know they weren't making it? —an added ignominy! "Why do you single me out? A week ago I didn't even know you—or do you just go around generally putting people on?" he said in a rush, hating the way he sounded—defensive, wary, intimidated. Why didn't he just tell the son of a bitch to go fuck himself.

The stony insolent expression seemed to soften, grow almost benign. Probably the closest the bastard ever came to a smile, Jules thought.

"You're mistaken, Friend, I'm not putting you on. I'm an observer of the human condition. I like to see people act with conviction. When I see them acting otherwise, in a vacillating or phony way, I try to be of service."

"I'm eternally indebted," Jules said, wincing at his own feeble sarcasm. He started to walk away.

"Oh, and Roman . . ."

He half turned, kept walking.

"If you find yourself at loose ends, the room in the Chinese hotel is still available."

"Fuck you," Jules said temperately over his shoulder.

* * *

At home he spread Cheez Whiz on the remains of the bread, devoured that and the tomato, and, still famished, hit the freezer compartment. No Kona coffee. Crazy; to be expected. Par for the past two days.

Restive, jiggy, needing to do something, he began to fill out his time report, and when the phone rang he answered it immediately.

"Where the devil you been, Jules?"

"Who were you in Dante's with?"

"Huh?"

"Last night."

"Oh . . . I didn't see you. Henry and me stopped in for some espresso. If you was there why didn't you come over?"

Jules exhaled metallically into the mouthpiece, covering his eyes with his hand.

"Jules?"

"Yes."

"You sound kind o' funny. I been tryin' to reach you for—What you been up to?"

"Nothing. In point of fact I'm rather down if you want to know the God's truth."

A pause on the other end.

"Are you still my friend?"

He couldn't help it, he began laughing, softly, helplessly.

"Jules, stop that now. . . . Please say somethin'."

"I'm still your friend."

"You are?"

"I just said so."

"Whew. I'm glad o' that. I been gettin' to work late

mornin's takin' the bus. Henry was good enough to take me yesterday."

"You should consider yourself honored."

"Huh?"

"Have you had your audition yet?" he said with an effort.

"Naw, it's been postponed. They're gonna call me."

"Par for the course."

"I don't like the way you sound, Jules. Are you comin' over here?"

"Yes."

"You are?"

"Didn't I just say so?"

"Okay. We'll have a little party or somethin'. Like make believe we haven't seen each other for a long time."

"Wild."

"When're you comin'?"

"Presently."

"Hey, Jules?"

"What?"

"Have you been a good boy?"

"Yes, Mammy," he said through clenched teeth and hung up.

He gazed at the ebony plate beside the door for a moment before knocking: c. BROWN 3-B. So innocuous.

When she opened the door his glance slid past her narrow face to where Henry, Reba Mae and Elmer were sitting on folding chairs around a card table sipping the California Sunburst Aperitif Wine. Welcome home.

My kingdom for a white face.

"Hey, you're a sight for sore eyes, Jules," Carmel said happily. "I guess you knows everybody here."

Henry, smiling cherubically, bobbed his head; Reba Mae and Elmer murmured low unintelligible sounds of greeting.

Jules nodded back, his heart in his stomach.

"Elmer was good enough to bring some chairs an' the table up. There's a chair for you there, Jules."

He sat down stiffly between Henry and Reba Mae, his mouth glued shut. The three pairs of eyes confronting him seemed hooded, malevolent. Seance on a dry evening.

"You want some wine, Jules?" Carmel said, breaking the silence.

"Please."

She poured some in a coffee mug and he took a grateful swallow, the stuff curling the back of his tongue, slipping down his throat like thin varnish.

"Guess what, Jules, I was just reading them my new poem." Carmel squeezed into the chair beside him.

"You're finished, I hope." He said it with a smile, trying to inject some levity into the proceedings.

"Aw . . ." Carmel's face began to crumple.

"I was joking. Go ahead and read it."

"It's a real snappy little poem," Henry said, pouring himself more of the Sunburst. " 'Course I don't pretends to understand it."

"I's all finished," Carmel said, sullen.

"Please read it again," Jules said, hearing something giddy and forlorn in his voice.

Carmel sat mute, petulant.

"Now you hurt her feelings," Reba Mae said with reproach.

"I really would like to hear the poem," Jules said, adamantly now, forcing conviction into his tone.

"Maybe we ought to play us some poker," Henry said. He took a deck of glossy-backed cards from his coat pocket and began shuffling them, humming a little tune to himself.

Elmer grunted assent. He looked older, somehow more substantial and dignified, and Jules suddenly realized why: This was the first time he had seen the man dressed in something other than his underwear.

"Little poker?" Henry said to Jules, still shuffling.

"I'm afraid I don't play."

The two men gazed at him in stolid disbelief.

"Just canasta and hearts. And a little bridge."

They kept staring at him. I appear to be in a distinct minority here, he thought giddily.

"You know what I feels like doin'?" Carmel said. "I feels like callin' my old man and seein' how Jo-jo is. I sure miss the little tyke."

"Yas, children can be a blessing," Reba Mae said, looking stoically across at Elmer.

"Waadoo, waadoo," Carmel crooned plaintively.

"We could teach you, no trouble," Henry said.

"Not tonight, thanks." Jules poured himself more of the Sunburst: already his stomach was kicking a bit of it up and there was a dull throbbing at the back of his skull. If this was the stuff the winos drank, small wonder they were found mornings slumped against buildings, unable to raise their heads. He said in a mild conversational tone to Henry, "How's the tire business?"

"Tolerably good. Could be better. People just ain't aware what they're missin' with these San Bruno bargains." His expression was benign; the affable cherubic face told nothing.

"I dreamt about my sister last night," Reba Mae said. "Walkin' cross the street toward me in the sun an' wearin' the same pretty blue dress we buried her in."

"Is that a fact," Carmel said.

"I saw the dress clearly as I see my own. Kind of a midnight blue, three-quarter sleeves an' ruffles."

"There's some sym-bo-lism connected there," Carmel said. "You look it up in the book I lent you."

"You think we might get Arthur for some lowball?" Elmer said.

"Worth a try." Henry blocked the cards neatly on the table and returned them to his pocket.

"That's my brother's name—Arthur," Jules said.

"This sure ain't your brother," Elmer said, his chest heaving with soundless mirth. He rose laboriously.

"How much money you carryin' in your pocket?" Reba Mae said sternly.

"There's no problem, woman." Elmer was standing now, looking down. "I guess we're gonna have to take this table."

Carmel removed the used glasses and half-gallon jug, and Elmer folded up the table and carried it to the door.

"Thankee for the wine 'n' everything," Henry said, standing. He bobbed his head at Jules.

"Okay, you welcome, Henry," Carmel said.

"Good night," Jules said, inanely raising his glass of Sunburst.

The door closed behind the two men, and Reba Mae heaved a ponderous sigh, signifying nothing.

"You want a drop more wine, Reba Mae?" Carmel said.

"No, I guess I better be movin' on downstairs."

"You lemme have that book back when you're through. There's this one I been havin' about Longwell. He's a mater dee in this swank cabaret wearin' a tuxedo, very smart and dapper, and all the white folk fawn on him except there's this one colored gal who sings with the band and she jus' won't give him the time o' day, nothin'."

"Huh," Reba Mae grunted; she gazed torpidly at Jules from beneath hooded lids.

The bottle was on the floor between his feet. Bending, he poured himself a full glass, then sipped slowly through fifteen more minutes of dream-and-analysis exchange.

Finally Reba Mae hove to, sighing, and waddled to the door. "G'night, honey. Elmer can pick up the chairs tomorrow."

"Pleasant dreams, Reba Mae."

She nodded to Jules. "Night." And pulled the door closed behind her.

"Ooeee, Reba Mae could sure stand takin' off some o' them excess pounds."

"Don't any of these people know my name?"

"'Course they do, Jules."

"I'm constantly addressed by nods, grunts and monosyllables."

"You have to give 'em time to get used to you is all. Now just where you been at these past two days?"

"Let's go to bed." He went to the door and fixed the chain fastener.

"There you go boltin' us in again. Two nights now I feel like I been out of jail. Now I's back in."

Wordlessly he started to undress. His stomach was sour and his skull felt encased in cement. Aperitif wine: Sunburst ought to be investigated for gross misrepresentation.

"Well, I can see you are *in*-communic*a*do tonight," Carmel said in her prissy highfalutin voice; hand testing her head for stray hairs, she sauntered into the bathroom.

He lay in bed listening to the barracks noises. It was still early. Overhead now someone was dragging loose bags of marbles around the floor.

Carmel came out of the bathroom and turned off the light. In her blue robe she knelt beside him. "I missed you, Jules. You're my baby."

He reached up and touched the sweet grave face. But all he could really see were the whites of her eyes.

"Jules—if you want, you can get under the bottom cover tonight."

"I'm already there."

"Oh."

She got in beside him. A door slammed somewhere. He breathed evenly, slowly, measuring the breaths.

"Waadoo, waadoo," Carmel crooned.

"What's that? You did it before."

"It's what Jo-jo used to do at night when he wanted water. Gee, I miss the little tyke."

He lay quietly, breathing more deeply now, tremulously.

"I forgot to draw the curtain, Jules. The moon's in my face. It's a bad sign."

He got up wordlessly, crossed the room and drew the kitchen curtains. When he came back he turned the covers aside and undid the belt of Carmel's robe. "You won't be requiring this accouterment any more," he said in a flat constricted voice: someone else's voice entirely.

"Naw, Jules . . . I didn't mean for you to—"

"I'm tired of this. I'm taking you, Miss Brown—no more intimidation."

"Jules, naw—" she shied back, whimpering—"I can't do nothin'. You're jus' my baby . . ."

"Don't worry. Everything's gonna be just everything." His voice was shaking, exultant, his heart slamming in his throat.

"Naw, Jules, please—wake up, wake up . . . Owow-owowowowow."

"Everything's all right. I love you."

Then silence; with movement. Her head was turned sideways; he looked once and thought he saw her grimacing in pain. When it was over he fell drained the relaxed on his side. "Jesus Christ, I think I actually love you," he heard himself say.

Without a sound Carmel suddenly began pummeling him with her fists and knees, the rapid rain of blows falling on his back and legs like a chastisement, a benediction. It went on for minutes, an undulating tattoo falling and rising in intensity, a masseur's rhythm. Gradually the blows abated and weakened. Panting heavily, Carmel dropped her hands and lay back. He waited a moment, then sat up and drew the covers gently over them. She came briefly to life again, thrashing about, kicking weakly against the covers, then abruptly subsiding with a little whimpering sound. He felt so very loose, boneless, voluptuously relaxed; peaceful and breathing easily. The air in the room was warm and sweet, like a balm. He saw that he hadn't drawn the curtains completely closed; a wafer of moon shone through. Carmel's breath quieted and steadied. He waited until it became the breath of sleep, then slipped out of bed and into his pants, shirt and shoes. Lightheaded, moving weightlessly, he unlatched the door and tiptoed downstairs, treading lightly as a sylph, out into the parking lot.

He unlocked his car and got the piece of chalk from the glove compartment.

I must be truly insane, he told himself, drawing fresh marks on the four tires by the light of the silvery moon.

Twelve

The next morning he dropped Carmel off early at Mrs. Cameron's and went home for a change of clothes. There was an envelope on his kitchen table; it contained the receipt for the month's rent he'd just paid and a typewritten note.

MR. ROMAN:

Commencing November 1 the rent for your apartment will be $95. Rising costs have necessitated this increase.

Thank you,
MRS. WILLIAMS, *Mgr.*

He went back downstairs and knocked on her door. Hard. No sound from within. He kept on knocking until he heard a soft padding of footsteps. The door opened, a quarter hitch. She was in slippers and a woolen bathrobe, the mottled gray hair slightly askew; pale morning light glinted coldly from her spectacles.

"It's very early, Mr. Roman."

"Mrs. Williams, what is this?" He held the note in his hand.

"Clearly just what it says."

"What costs have risen specifically?"

"Maintenance and utilities. I've warned you before

about your lights."

"That amounts to a few pennies. You're gouging me, Mrs. Williams."

"You're a rude and uncivil young man."

"I'm moving out," he announced, trying to control the tremor in his voice. "Today if I can manage it."

"You're certainly free to do so. Excuse me a moment."

Through the partly open door he watched her poke around in a cubbyhole of the old-fashioned desk. She returned with a sheet of paper. He took it from her, gazing in disbelief at the heading:

TERMINAL INVENTORY BILL
Mr. Roman

Fantastic. She'd anticipated him. His eyes swept over the typewritten items.

Bal. rent due on required week's notice of intention to vacate	$20.00
Bal. due from previous bill (*bathroom damage*)	7.75
Vacancy cleaning charge 2 rms	6.00
Breakage or missing:	
2 *cups*	.50
1 *drinking glass*	.20
1 *kitchen knife*	.60
1 *saucer*	.15
	$35.20
Security deposit applied hereto	35.00
BALANCE DUE	$ .20

"I owe you twenty cents."

"That's correct."

"If you can produce the missing kitchen knife, Mrs. Williams, why don't you simply cut my heart out and get it over with."

"I don't intend to stand here and listen to your rudeness."

"Or even more expedient, slit my throat."

The door closed softly in his face.

Scarcely to be believed.

Trembling with anger, he went upstairs. You'll get your twenty cents, Mrs. Williams, never fear. You'll get yours all right.

He phoned Mrs. Cameron's residence, asked to speak with Miss Brown; shaking the water from his head.

"Hullo?" She answered cautiously; he'd called her there only once before.

"It's me."

"Hey, Jules . . ."

"May I stay with you for a few days?"

"Well, sure—"

"I mean *stay*. Bag and baggage. I've been evicted."

"Why'd they do that?"

"I'll explain later. I should be able to find a place in a few days. But if this is going to inconvenience you, say so."

"Naw, you come on over . . . if you're sure you really wants to."

"I really *want* to. For Christ's sake, Carmel!"

"Huh?"

He drew a steadying breath, lowered his voice. "I want to. Look, I'm very fond of you, and last night I

. . . If it's all right I'll move in this morning. We'll have some furniture, a table and chairs, lamp . . ."

"Okay. I'll bring some fresh cream home tonight."

"You're a dear old soul, Carmel."

"Uh-huh."

"Not to say a kindred spirit."

"Okay."

He hung up, got his suitcases out of the closet. Don't think about anything, just pack. Get out, away from that woman. Blood-sucking frigid old hag. The furniture would have to wait until later; he'd need help for that. He paused, sweating, called the office and told the woman to tell Mergy he was taking the morning off. Emergency.

An hour later, heart pounding, he had everything piled in the Plymouth. Done and done. Another trip across the wide Missouri.

Reba Mae, hearing bags banging against the stairway walls, opened her door.

"Plannin' on stayin'?"

"Just for a few days."

Using his key, he banged his way in, dumping everything in the middle of the floor.

She was still there as he struggled up with the second load.

"Bag 'n' baggage, huh?"

"Yep." *Don't offer to help, Reba. Just stand there on the sidelines with your fat ass sticking out, cheering me on. Yassuh.*

The third load—suits, jackets, blankets—did it. Dripping sweat, exhausted, he got undressed and under the shower, reveling in the stinging downward spray and unaccustomed stand-up position—suddenly remembering he'd left his shower attachment in its closet hiding place. Crazy, let it go; one more lifeline severed; goddam bridges burning all over town.

At seven o'clock, a rented U-haul van hooked to the rear bumper of the Plymouth, he returned with Henry for the furniture. He found his first shower attachment, the pale-green one she'd appropriated, neatly coiled on the kitchen table. Illegally entering to the end. He swept the thing onto the floor, where it leisurely unwound like a snake.

Mrs. Williams came out of her ground-floor apartment as they struggled down with the solid-oak table. "Careful of the banister, please."

Jules kept his mouth clamped shut. Twenty cents, Mrs. Williams. I won't forget that.

"Please be careful," she said as Henry lurched into the newel post, the old wood groaning. "What company do you work for, young man?"

"He's not company, he's a friend," Jules said between clenched teeth.

"Yes, *sir*," Henry said.

Carmel was watching TV, cross-legged on the mattress, chin cupped in her palms. Everything was moved in. He had thanked Henry and offered him a couple of dollars, which the little fellow had graciously refused, bobbing his head and wishing him a pleasant night's sleep.

"You can sit on a chair now," he said.

"This is okay, Jules," she said, watching Ray Milland

pop fruit from a grocery stand into the paper bag full of booze bottles.

"Can we call it an early night? I'm done in."

"Yeah, I just wanna see the part again where the bat and the mouse come outa the wall. Pow!"

"I feel the need of another shower, all right?"

"You just go right on ahead, Jules."

In the bathroom he got undressed and under the shower, feeling at once bone-weary and exhilarated. He should have taken this step weeks ago. What a good cathartic feeling it had been telling off that miserable bitch. In the future he wouldn't let himself be intimidated by such people. Twenty cents! And without batting an eye. Jesus, what gall. Well, he was free of that entanglement; no more white uniform and brass key ring. Free. Tomorrow, Saturday, he'd look for an apartment, but in the interim . . . Henry really wasn't such a bad little guy refusing that two bucks. (Could he have been wrong about the tire?) In the interim he had a reasonably comfortable place, TV, shower, lissome Miss Brown in the next room. He wondered if he should hit on her again in bed. She really seemed to have been in pain last night. Could it have been the first time for her? Fantastic. More likely she'd just never had the right experience; probably someone in the past had botched the job badly. He'd be gentle with her, considerate, patient . . . Fleetingly he wished Gloria were in the shower with him, bumping asses dilly dilly, soaping each other slowly, lovingly *I think that's enough on that particular spot, that'll do just fine Roman, thank you* . . . Jesus, Art should see him now, Carmel squatting like an Indian in the next room, Henry, Elmer, Reba

Mae on all sides. He wouldn't believe it. And Mary's eyes would bug with shock, her plump little face quivering, ashen. Dear old Mary. Outerbridge Horsey, our man in Czechoslovakia. A grand old name . . .

He thought he heard Carmel calling, shut off the water and stuck his head out the door. "What?"

"I'm just tellin' whoever's at the door to hang on. Bangin' away t' beat the band . . ." She was up, crossing the room.

He pulled the bathroom door almost shut, his skin suddenly, inexplicably crawling, listening at the crack. Over the unnerving mouse-bat squealing from the TV he heard Carmel cry out, "Longwell!" Then peevish, irritable, scolding, "Where the devil you been?"

Thirteen

The drapes in Henry's apartment were drawn. A cone of hot light from the top bullet of a brass pole lamp shone on the oblong dining-room table.

"I have two pair," Jules said, laying down his cards. "Kings and nines."

"But you see that don't beat three of a kind no matter how low." Henry gathered in the chips. "You're learnin', though."

"What's that draft board do if they catch up with you?" Elmer said to Longwell.

"Man, I do not even want to think about it."

"They took my brother-in-law's nephew last month," Henry said. "Lifted him straight out of this nice operation he had going in Oakland. Bar-supply business."

Longwell shuffled rapidly and dealt four hands. "I was pretty well situated down south, then that notice came and I thought, man, I can't get shot full of holes at my age. If they find me they'll have to truss me up and drag my ass down the stairs. And I'll be kicking all the way."

Jules found himself oddly attracted to Longwell, though aware that the feeling was grounded in a strong sense of relief. His initial apprehension—Longwell's reaction to his sister living with a paddy—had been unfounded; he had accepted Jules' presence matter-of-factly, even indifferently. Last night Jules had sat in his robe while Carmel fed her brother and he explained about the induction notice instigating his abrupt departure from Los Angeles. Having heard from Julius that she was in San Francisco, he caught a Greyhound bus and found her address in the phone book. Brother and sister looked strikingly alike, the same taut grave features, Longwell taller and somewhat lighter-skinned. His eyes, like Carmel's, were deep brown and somber but there was a peculiar light, an intelligence, in them, something keen and furtive. Under a mohair jacket he wore a dark woolen sweater cut off at the shoulders in lieu of a shirt. His smile was guileless and affectionate as he replied to Carmel's "What was you doin' down there? I dreamt you was a mater dee in a plush cabaret."

"Nothing quite so fancy. You're dreaming again, Charcoal."

"You shut up with that name."

"Hee-haw," Longwell said mildly.

"Dummy, I been lookin' all over the wrong town for you. Are you gonna want to stay here?"

"Well, I'll need some place to lay dead. Temporarily."

Jules' heart sank.

"Lemme call Henry first. He got a divan up there."

"By the way, if anyone comes asking about me, you know from nothing. You haven't seen or heard from me in years."

"*Uh*-huh, an' that's near the truth," Carmel said, lifting the phone.

Henry, to Jules' vast relief, was amenable.

Longwell said now, scrutinizing his cards, "I'm going to need some kind of job."

"Maybe I can do something for you at the hotel," Elmer said.

"You sure are funny," Henry said. "Here's a boy on the brink of his life, he don't want to be standing 'round no toilet." Henry turned to the others, his round cherubic face gleaming. "You should see him in that toilet on Nob Hill whiskin' away, the speediest broom on the Hill—then tucking them match books in the customer's pockets. 'Here you go, sir, they's free, take some home to the wife and kiddies,' " Henry mimicked.

"Let's cut out all the guff and play the game," Elmer said.

"What happens with this guy O'Hara my sister mentioned?" Longwell said.

"Be careful of him," Jules said.

"Man, I am careful of *every*body these days."

Henry, fanning his cards close to the chest, recited in a singsong voice, " 'Have you heard it's in the stars, next July we collides with Mars . . .' Hit me with a goody," he said, slapping a card down; and to Longwell, "I got a few possibilities in mind I'll talk to you about later."

At the end of the hand Elmer said, "Let's get on to the money."

Henry turned to Jules. "You feel ready?"

"I guess—reasonably."

"That's a mighty big word for yes or no," Elmer said.

"Well now he used to be a school teacher, didn't you know?" Henry said affably.

Twenty minutes later Jules was down a dollar and a half, sweating lightly. The phone rang.

Henry reached behind him. "Henry here . . . Yas, just hold on a minute." He covered the mouthpiece. "It's Carmel. She says come on downstairs now and stop losin' all your money."

Jules gathered up his cards. "Tell her a half hour."

Relieved of four dollars and seventy-five cents, he went back downstairs, Henry's "Have yourself a pleasant night's sleep" lingering in his ears.

Carmel was already in bed. "How much you lose?"

He went for the refrigerator.

"Go on, scarf up all the cream. I guess them boots took every penny."

When he was through he dropped the carton in the garbage pail and got undressed in the dark. Padded across the cold floor in his bare feet to check the door.

"You stop that rattlin' now. I never seen anyone so fearful. Nevah in all m' born days . . ." Carmel trailed off, sighing.

Sliding under the covers, he slipped his hand inside the blue robe. Her breasts felt the way he'd always imagined a young Filipino girl's would feel: small, firm, protuberant; brown and hard as walnuts.

"Cut it out now, you gonna give me cancer. . . . What's so funny 'bout that?" She stopped his hand as it slid down over her belly, flat, marble-smooth. "Now I don't want you gettin' mad, Jules, but I can't do nothin' tonight."

Suddenly oppressed, dog-tired, he fell back on his pillow.

"You ain't mad, are you?"

He didn't answer.

"Jules, I forgot to draw the curtains again."

"Don't the moon look lonesome shining through the trees."

"Yeah," Carmel said.

"Why are you so sexless."

A long silence. He wished he could retract it—or rephrase it.

"I's sexless 'cause I got done in up north."

"How do you mean?"

"Done in. This old fat paddy up at the ranch cottages. See this?" He watched, fascinated: She was holding her middle finger straight up in the moonlight.

"What about it?"

" 'You know where it's goin',' " he said. " 'Warm you up.' "

"Then what happened?"

"He did me in. Everythin'."

Jules blinked. "Didn't you tell anyone?"

"You're the first."

They lay silently, swathed in moonlight. It seemed a whiter, colder light than that which shone through the second-floor bedroom window in Willimouth.

"Why didn't you tell me before?" he said, wondering if she could be inventing the story. Not likely; she wasn't that imaginative. *You know where it's goin'. Warm you up.*

"It's not something I'd be *in*clined to bring up in po-lite conversation," she said with a slight Mrs. Cameron inflection.

"Others girls get done in and get over it. You shouldn't let it affect your whole life."

"Well, I needs more time. I love havin' you here, Jules, but if you're gonna be feelin' this way every night you better find yourself some vitamin F."

"Vitamin F!"

"That's what I calls it."

"Marvelous. Wouldn't that bother you?"

"Huh?"

"If I got it elsewhere."

"Mmm . . . I guess. A little." She sat up.

"Now what?"

"I got to shut out the moon."

At the window, reaching for the curtains, her face and arms fleetingly steeped in a moonbath: bronze bathed silver.

Back under the covers, she said, "Jules, do you think I might borrow your jalop tomorrow? It's Sunday and Longwell and I thought we'd like to drive north to see the fam'ly."

"Can he drive?"

"Sure—I think. I'd be careful. I'm good behind the wheel, Jules."

"You dreamin' again, Charcoal."

"I'm gonna bite your face." She beat a rapid tattoo on his arm with her tiny fists, legs pumping.

Jules turned over with a sigh, his nose inches from the wooden floor, wondering how much beds cost at the Goodwill stores. Jesus, what a long way from the green fields of Connecticut. Running barefoot in the dew-cold grass.

"I jus' hope the draft board don't catch Longwell," she said after a time. "He'd be no good in the army. No good at-all."

But Jules had drifted off.

He was being shaken like a mouse in a cage. He came out of it damp with sweat, gray light filling the room.

"What . . ."

"You was mumblin' away, Jules, talkin' to Mrs. Wilson. 'You'll get your effin' twenty cents, Mrs. Wilson, you'll get it . . .' "

"You're mad."

"I'm tellin' you, Jules. You were mumblin' and rantin' away. Who's Mrs. Wilson?"

"Williams . . . Are you sure?"

"Yeah. When you dreams about money it means you're expectin' a reward or—"

"I know what it means. It means I owe that miserable old bag twenty cents. Jesus, I never used to dream this much until I met you."

"Uh-huh." Carmel nodded her head sagely. "Next time just say to yourself, Wake up, wake up."

"What time is it?"

"Gettin' on past seven o'clock. You gonna let me take the car like you said last night?"

"I was going to look for an apartment today," he hedged.

"Aw, you don't have to do that. You stay here awhile. I really got myself set on seein' Jo-jo and the fam'ly, Jules."

"You've got to be careful. It's my neck if anything happens."

"We'll just barely creep along, Jules, I promise." Grateful, jubilant, she cradled his head in her arms, kissing his face all over, nose, eyes, ears, nibbling like a hare with appropriate mastication sounds. "I loves ya, Jules. You're my baby." She drew back a few inches, her eyes huge, peering into his. "You want to come along with us?"

"I decline. Respectfully."

"Okay." She scrambled up, went for the pile of newspapers under the sink, expertly furled a page and lit the end. Resigned, he watched the operation, set himself for the ominous blammmm of igniting gas, but he was never completely prepared; it always hit him with an unexpected jolt. If she waited too long, if too much gas built up, the cardboard walls reverberated as from a sonic boom.

She doused the torch under the sink faucet and came back to bed. Already he could feel the heat pouring from the open oven.

"You're far away, ain't you, Jules? What you thinkin'?"

"There's a road sign in Connecticut going into New York that says, 'Sho-Nuff, Northern Fried Chicken.'"

"Is that a fact?"

"It's a fact."

She pulled the covers up to her neck, squirming comfortably. "Hey, Jules, I'm gonna take tomorrow mornin' off to finish my new poem, then I'm comin' down and have lunch with you."

"I'm not sure exactly when I'll be free."

She gave a tiny elfin smile, delighted with her ruse.

"Uh-huh, I know. You're ashamed to take me any place."

"I didn't say that—"

"Supposin' I just sashayed down to that office aroun' noon and said, 'I's heah to see Mistuh Roman.' What would they say, Jules?"

"Mistuh Roman, he don't work heah no mo."

"Ah, Jules, you crack me up." Grinning, pleased, she began nibbling at his face again, rubbing his belly with a rapid rotary motion. "You really cracks me up."

Fourteen

"You should have let me know as soon as you moved. We mailed you the new materials a week ago." Mergy had just returned from five days in the Midwest.

"I notified the post office. I assumed my mail would be forwarded."

"Well it obviously hasn't been. What number Pacific?"

"Nine seventy-five, I think. Havila Apartments."

Mergy's pencil stopped in mid-number; he looked up. "Near Chinatown? Four-story white wooden building?"

"That's it."

"Isn't it rather dark over there?"

"It's integrated," Jules said; the word almost came out "in-tee-grated." "We're all born equal, Mr. Mergy," he added inadvisedly.

"I don't require a lecture on civil rights, Roman. I don't give a toot in hell where you live so long as you do your job. I'm merely wondering out loud what sends a boy of your background to that section of town."

"The rent," Jules said, his mind reverting to the crumpled rear fender of the Plymouth parked two blocks away, token of Carmel's recent excursion up north ("We was barely creepin' along, Jules, an' this old fart came outa the blue . . ."). No voucher this time; he'd have to have it repaired on his own. "Is that all?" he said, making a motion toward the door.

"Unfortunately, no."

Jules stopped, met Mergy's flat blue eyes. Ice on ice. "Unfortunately . . ."

"As you know from your instruction sheet we now and then run accuracy checks on each interviewer's work via these double-return postcards." Mergy held up the item in question. "Mrs. Martinez," he read, "on Hunters Point Boulevard indicates that you showed her only three of the four magazine issues. Yet your report shows a completed interview at that address."

Shot down again.

"I can't really recall the exact—"

"It's the sort of thing that undermines the validity of our entire program. Don't fall into that kind of trap, Roman." Incredibly, Mergy now winked at him; a sly grin transformed the broad blunt features. "We'll consider it a temporary corrected fall from grace, *comprends?*"

"I understand," Jules said, acknowledging the fall. Jesus, the organization is going to crumble because a sad old lady scarcely able to speak the English language, much less read it, does not get to pass judgment on a ten-month-old copy of *Look*. Crazy.

"Jean and I would like to have you drop by for dinner next week if you're free, Roman."

Unbelievable.

"Fine," he said dazedly.

"Any particular night best?"

No way out. "It doesn't matter."

"Shall we say Wednesday, six-thirty?"

"Fine."

Mergy turned back to his paperwork.

"Good night," Jules said.

Engrossed, Mergy nodded.

You never really do know what's coming off next, Jules thought, driving home. What possible reason could Mergy have for inviting him to dinner? After catching him with his hand practically in the till. A temporary *corrected* fall from grace, he'd said. Crazy. Then the casual turn-around had caught him completely off guard. Jean and I would like to have you drop by . . . He pictured Jean: diminutive, harried-looking, a perpetual bright pained smile; graying steadily at the temples.

On Grant Avenue a Sale-on-Prints sign caught his eye. Something to cover the barracks walls; the blankness was driving him mad. He found a parking spot beside a hydrant, left an Emergency note on the windshield and went in. Torn between a Modigliani nude and a Van Gogh landscape, he decided on the latter. Carmel would want to cover up the girl's crotch.

In the Havila parking lot he saw Longwell and Henry stacking tires on the back of Henry's pickup. Henry waved to him. "We got some business. Be back in a hour or so." Jules nodded, locked the car and went upstairs.

Carmel was standing before a small face mirror propped on the TV set, drawing thick wiry strands of her hair straight up. For a startling moment she looked to Jules like something out of the jungle. Only the thatched hut and tom-tom were missing. Now she dipped her fingers into an open jar of a whitish gooey substance.

"What's going on?"

"Tryin' to sleek it down. This gal next door to Mrs. C showed me." She grimaced, laying the goo into the strands of thick hair with the heels of her palms. "You paddies don't know how lucky you are." In the mirror she watched him unroll the print. "What you got, Jules, a present for me?"

"You might say that." He held it stretched out on his chest.

"Ooeee, that's pretty. Did you do it?"

He looked at her in dismay. "It's by a fellow named Van Gogh."

"Oh . . . That's the man you told me looked like O'Hara."

"If I'd remembered that I would have got the Modigliani."

"Huh?"

"What's for dinner?"

"Chicken, northern-fried. And don't get mad, Jules, I forgot the cream for dessert."

"No matter, I'll run out and get some watermelon."

Wary, she watched him in the mirror. "I don't like you talkin' like that. I can't ever tell when you're jokin'. You gettin' awful jiggy again lately."

"Don't you know why?" He came up behind her, cupped the Filipino-maiden's breasts in his hands.

"I'm gonna tell." She kept on with her hair; it smelled vile from the grease. "I don't want you gettin' this way. We did it Tuesday."

"Not enough." Inflamed, he squeezed the walnut

breasts, sunk his teeth gently into the rich chocolate throat.

"Owowow. You gonna give me cancer. I can't do anythin' for a while, Jules, I'm not right."

He removed his teeth from her throat, keeping hold of the breasts. "What does that mean?"

"I got a kind of problem down there. Mrs. C's gonna send me to her doctor."

"You're lying, Charcoal."

"You shut up!" In the mirror her face crumpled like a child's. "You wanna *see?*"

"Not before dinner, thanks." He released her, went into the kitchen. Feverish, fuming with frustration, he got down his bottle of King George IV Scotch from the cabinet over the sink. Not the world's most elegant whiskey but a few cuts above the Sunburst Aperitif. He poured himself a heavy one on the rocks, then rummaged in the drawers until he found the tacks he'd seen a week ago. Using the base of a coffee mug as a hammer, he laid the Van Gogh savagely into the bare wall.

Wrapping her head in a towel, Carmel studied the print. "Yeah, that's sure pretty." She bent over, peering at the inscription. "Less vessels . . ."

" 'Les Vessenots à Auvers'!" Jules yelled.

"Oh. What's it mean?"

"Vessenots . . . What the—cottages? Fields? I'm not sure. Auvers is a town in France. Just look at it and enjoy it."

"That's what I'm doin', dummy." After a quarter minute's silent appraisal, she said, "Don't play poker tonight, Jules. We'll have a nice easy dinner lookin' at the picture and then watch telly. I don't want you losin' any more money."

"This present trend can't continue. But if it does, your brother and Henry can use the capital. Did you know they're in business together now?"

"Yeah."

"The tire business," he said.

"Uh-huh."

"If the draft board doesn't get Longwell, the local boys in blue will."

"Don't say that." Eyeballs rolled upward, she pinned the folds of the towel together. "You 'n' Longwell's about the same age. How come you ain't drafted?"

"I have a deviated septum," he said with as much dignity as he could muster.

"Oh. What the devil's that?"

"My nose is all screwed up. Inside."

She stared at it. "Is that a fact?"

"It's a fact. I wish you'd wash your hands—that stuff really stinks."

"I'm gonna." She screwed the cap back on the grease jar and wiped her hands on a sheet of newspaper. "I called the people today I was supposed to audition for. They said they'd made other co-mitments. They prob'ly don't take colored anyhow."

"In show business? You're dreaming, Charcoal."

"You shut up."

He went into the kitchen and poured another Scotch. "What, and give up show business?" he murmured, re-membering only the tag line of an old joke.

"Jules, what's seepy?"

"What?"

"This magazine piece I was readin' today said Barbra

Streisand's like a seepy Lena Horne."

"Sepia!" he yelled, breaking up.

"Stop makin' fun o' me. I'm gonna bite your face.
. . . What's it mean?"

"Brown!"

"Oh."

Jules shook his head, grinning delightedly. "A seepy Lena Horne . . . Jesus, that's priceless."

"You just keep on keepin' on like that, laugh your shit head off!" Tight-lipped, scowling fiercely, she stomped into the bathroom.

Sound of drumming water against tin shower walls, splashing over a naked body. His heart, accelerating fast, began hammering. Christ, I'm in heat. He waited another moment or two, then took off all his clothes, stealthily opened the bathroom door and tiptoed in. He drew aside the curtain. The sleek streaming brown body against the white towel-wound head was something to behold.

Carmel jumped, eyes huge, backing resoundingly against the tin wall. "What the devil . . ."

"I'll soap you up," he said, stepping in.

"You ain't soapin' nothin' up! Get out!"

The deflected spray was spurting into his eyes. "Take it easy, I'm just—"

She gave him a shove that sent him halfway through the curtain. "Dodo, get out!"

"You stupid boot . . ."

"Paddy. Shithead. Get outa here!"

Muttering to himself, streaming water, he retreated to the other room. Banged his fist in a weak rage against the Van Gogh, and, turning slowly, warily, found himself confronting Elmer standing in the doorway.

"I knocked but there was no . . ." Elmer's hooded gaze dropped briefly down the wet naked length of him, then back up to the face. "I was wonderin' if there was a game on tonight."

An hour and a half later, Henry, raking in his third consecutive pot, chanted in singsong "'. . . She got pinched in the Ass-tor bar, Well-did-you-evah . . .'" And Longwell, looking Jules dead in the eye, said quietly, completely out of the blue, "Are you planning to marry my sister?"

Fifteen

The following week he lent her one hundred and thirty dollars, a sizable chunk out of his savings, to buy a car. Henry and Longwell had found a "one-in-five-hundred bargain" in a used-car lot on Mission Street—a light-green 1953 Dodge with "surprisingly sound tires," Henry had observed. Carmel was jubilant. "I'm gonna work real hard to pay you back, Jules, work my fingers to the bone," she said, smothering his face with kisses. An added gratuity was the license plate: ZAP 707. "Rich folk'd pay good bread for a license like that," Henry observed. The four of them took a trial run around North Beach, going a good three blocks in sluggish, stuttering fashion until Longwell, leaning over the front seat, said, "You got the hand brake on, Charcoal."

Now, returning from dinner with Mergy and his wife, Jules thought, It will be a long hot summer before I see that hundred and thirty again, but he had no kicks coming. Each week he dutifully offered her money toward the rent; she wouldn't touch it. "You're my baby, Jules, and you got that deviated septic. I can't take no money." Crazy. Meanwhile her baby was getting his ass drubbed nightly by the upstairs poker clique. Yet even that was preferable to the abysmal loneliness of his first few weeks in the city. And he could always up and leave. Just a matter of gathering bag and baggage, piling the works back into another U-haul and taking off for one of the Caucasian hills.

It had been a strange evening at Mergy's. Over the pre-dinner drink Mergy had said, twirling the cubes in his glass, "You know, I'm not really an ogre, Jules," the Christian name used for the first time ringing oddly in the small Swedish-decor living room. This statement had been followed by a resounding silence, broken by Mrs. Mergy: "Walter has told me so much about you I feel as if we know each other. I can appreciate how difficult it must be to come to a new city from so far away without contact or friends . . ." He'd been dead wrong in his physical conception of Jean. She was big-boned, a heavy graceless woman with some warmth but not a glimmer of humor in her face; she looked like the headmistress of a Southern girls' academy. He couldn't imagine Mergy's invitation had stemmed from compassion or concern for his welfare; he just wasn't the type ("I don't give a toot in hell where you live," he remembered). As if bearing this out, Mergy, during dinner, had lightly broached the subject of a potential future beyond field work with Andrew Sylvester Research: perhaps after another year or so in a supervisory capacity, starting as field instructor—showing fledgling interviewers the ropes. They considered themselves fortunate to have a college graduate in the ranks, and his teaching experience would prove invaluable. Why had he decided to leave teaching? . . . Goaded by a demon, he'd been tempted to answer, Some of my girl students were turning me on. "Discipline was my *bête noire*," he said, perversely undermining Mergy's faith in the value of his teaching experience.

"Your—?"

"*Bête noire.*"

He'd left as soon after dinner as was civilly possible.

He found himself inordinately eager to get back to the barracks, praying Carmel would be home. The entire troupe had gone to a party at O'Hara's pad over Dante's Coffeehouse, and if he got away early enough and no one was at Havila, he was supposed to drop by. Well, it was only ten-fifteen, but it would be a long day's journey into night before he'd step foot over that arrogant pimp's doorsill. I entreat you, Black Beauty, be home . . . Frigid, accident-prone, obscure poetess and compulsive liar—but that sweet antic mind and Filipino-maiden's body hung him up every time. Hope beats eternal. Then why at times did he deliberately try to hurt her? If only they had some semblance of sex life. *I do love you, Jules, but I can't do nothin' tonight.* Weird. Maybe he ought to suggest a psychiatric consultation.

ZAP 707 was not in the parking lot. He went upstairs and knocked on Henry's door, hoping the little fellow or Longwell might have come home early and they could play some two- or three-handed poker. There was no answer.

Despondent, restless, he went back downstairs, turned on the TV and shut it off immediately when he saw Jane Darwell rocking on the back porch of a ramshackle farmhouse out of the Thirties. He put on the new Lena Horne LP Carmel had bought and began leafing through her autograph album, stopping at a page that read

Jules
   Jo-jo (sepia)
   My babys

Count the moons of jupitor
Thousands of eyes in the skys

He closed the album, poured a heavy King George
IV and water, drank it off and went to bed.

Hours later he woke to tinkling music: Carmel stumbling among the coat hangers. By faint moonlight he
watched her try to slip her coat on one.

"Are you loaded?"

"*Ahhhhnn. . . !*" Her hands flew over her head; the
coat dropped. "I thought you was asleep."

"How's my *bête noire*?"

"Huh?"

"How was the party?"

"It was okay. Until a while ago." She stooped for the
coat, sinking onto one knee, coming up slowly.

"You're loaded."

"Well, yeah, jus' a tiny bit tipsy."

"What happened a while ago?"

"Mmm, O'Hara put on some dirty movies. They was
really somethin' else. Pos'tively *in*decent," she said, trying for the upper-class-Caucasian accent. "Really, Jules,
they was perfectly vile, disgus—"

"Then why did you stay?"

"Well we all came in the one car and the others
didn't want t' go just yet." She got her coat on a hanger,
came over and knelt down beside him, her face inches

from his, eyes clear agates. "*Je t'adore.*"

"What? It's shut."

"*Je t'adore.* This French girl at the party taught me. It means I adores you."

"It sounded like you were saying shut the door."

"Dummy." She straightened up, unbuttoning her dress, weaving slightly. "They was sure some strange gals there. Pow! One of 'em, Caucasian—a cute l'il gray babe—plopped herself on Longwell's lap an' started foolin' around somethin' fierce."

"They were probably all hookers. You might have been the only straight chick there."

"Aw, that's silly, Jules."

"O'Hara's a pimp. Surely you knew that."

"I don't know nothin' about it. You shouldn't say those things. He's a painter. There's these kind o' peculiar paintings all over the walls and he signs 'em T. Riley O'Hara. I didn't understand 'em though. I like our vessels picture better."

"Did any of the Caucasian men come on to you?"

"'Course not, dodo. I wouldn't let 'em. But O'Hara said to Reba Mae—" Carmel stuffed knuckles in her mouth, giggling— "said, 'Reba, let's you and me crawl into my sleepin' bag later on,' and Reba Mae, she was pretty fogged up with the wine, yells, 'Won't fit!' Then she dropped down to the floor and began walkin' on her knees makin' these strange honkin' noises like a goose. Cracked everybody up."

"A swell party, all told."

"Yeah. You close your eyes now and I'll be back in a sec. Get outa these ac-*cou*terments." She went into the bathroom and emerged minutes later in the electric-blue pajamas he'd bought for her. Wraithlike she advanced on him, a veritable brown-and-blue fantasy, phosphorescing.

"Chicken Little, I is beat." Sighing, she got in beside him.

He slid out from under the covers.

"You promised not to bolt it any more."

"I'm not boltin' nothin'," he said, inadvertently, smiling in half surprise at the cadence of her boot inflection in his tone. "I'm shutting out the moon for you." He started to draw the curtains and saw, in the parking lot below, Henry and Longwell hunched elflike in moonlight over the rear tire of a car. The Plymouth. His stomach took a wild turn. Skin crawling, he found his pants, pulled them on, stubbed his toes painfully getting into the loafers.

"Jules, what the devil you doin'?"

He grabbed his raincoat off the hanger and hurried out the door, down the steps two at a time, but carefully, making sure of his footing, feeling weirdly limber and resilient as if his bones were embedded in coil spring.

Coat flapping, he came out into the parking lot. They were using a wrench on one of the tires.

"What the hell are you guys doing?" His voice cracked like a boy's in the crisp night air.

Henry whispered hoarsely, "Let's go man, retreat . . . Oh, it's Jules."

The chill air swept through the open coat, freezing the sweat on his body. "I . . . thought it was *my* Plymouth."

"No problem, man," Longwell said.

From twenty feet away they gazed stolidly at him.

"Why are you guys screwing around?" His voice still humiliatingly out of control.

"Now, Jules, you don't know what you're saying," Henry said. "You don't know from anything."

"Just stay away from my car."

"Go back to bed, man. No one's bothering your car," Longwell said.

A head popped out of an upstairs window. Elmer.

"What's the problem down there?"

One tier above, like heads in a Punch and Judy show, Carmel's somber face appeared at the slightly parted curtains.

"No problems," Henry called up affably. "Everything's in control down here. Have a pleasant night's sleep."

Elmer's head slowly receded; the window came down.

"You're better off doing me in at poker. At least it's legal."

"Now, Jules, you really don't know what you're saying. And you're going to catch your death out here."

"Go back to bed, man. My sister's getting nervous."

He turned and walked away, hands deep in the pockets of the coat. Shivering as the sweat dried on his arms and chest. His skin felt as if it were encrusted with a frozen scum. Stiffly up the stairway he went like a zombie.

"What the devil was that all about?" Carmel said.

Without a word he stripped off the coat and pants and went into the bathroom, latching the door behind him. Ran the shower scalding hot, soaping himself luxuriously. Sweet-scented yellow soap melting under the cascade, tin-drumming water deliciously crashing his ears, drowning his senses.

Gloria.

Carmel rattling, banging on the bathroom door, shouting something.

Walter and Jean would get a kick out of this little tableau.

"*Jules!* . . . *What you* . . ."

Drowning her out, singing high and clear:

Some to make hay, dilly dilly, some to cut corn
While you and I, dilly dilly, keep ourselves warm!

Sixteen

A pokerless week passed. The others were civil enough to him, greeting him on the stairway, giving no indication that the parking-lot episode had ever occurred. But poker invitations were not forthcoming; he refused to put himself in the position of entreating a game, he wouldn't give them that satisfaction. And Black Beauty was acting stranger than usual—or was it his imagination? Several times he'd found her looking at him oddly, standing in the archway between the two rooms or gazing silently at him through the partly open bathroom door as he shaved, her face doleful, grave. Of course she may not have even been *seeing* him; you never quite knew what was going on in Miss Brown's mind. Strange. One evening after work as he was locking the car, he glanced intuitively up and saw her at the window, partly veiled by the curtains, gazing down at him: rapt, austere, mysterioso. And when their eyes met she abruptly stuck out her tongue and shook her tiny fist at him in mock belligerence. Weird.

Surrounded, listless, his will seemingly undermined by the presence of superior numbers, he told himself he at least had to make an effort to find an apartment. He spent Saturday afternoon following up leads in the *Chronicle* classified section, found nothing decent under a hundred dollars, and, relieved, came back to the barracks. Hungering for a white face all these weeks, prophetically he found her lugging a suitcase up the stairway.

"May I give you a hand?"

"You certainly *may*." She lowered the suitcase and sank back against the wall, blowing air up into her face. Short and pert, dark-haired; small even features except for a pronounced and somehow provocative bump just below the bridge of her nose; separating the wide light gray eyes, it gave her an angular, exotic look.

He lifted the suitcase. It was brick heavy. "Where to?"

"Two more floors. Four-E."

Down the hall from Henry; it had been vacant ever since he could remember.

"I'm Jules Roman."

"Trudy Lester. I'm a friend of Dori O'Hara's. She says she knows you."

Fifteen bucks, drinks, cab fare and a hound's-tooth sport coat, he remembered. His heart sank. Two months in this fabled town and he had met no one but hustlers, boots, and middle-aged housewives, most of them in "disadvantaged" areas. If Dori went for fifteen, this one, using an aesthetic measuring stick, should command twenty to twenty-five. But then why set up shop in Havila? It didn't figure. Controlling an urge to ask, How much? he said, "How did you find the apartment—through O'Hara?"

She gave him a brief sidelong look. "Indirectly."

Four-E was a replica of Carmel's apartment, barren of furniture. He lugged in the suitcase.

"I'd invite you in for coffee but as you can see I'm not prepared. You'll have to take a rain check."

His eyes roamed the muscular little body. Probably excellent vitamin F. "I guess I'll be running into you."

"I wouldn't be surprised." Cool gray eyes direct and unblinking. "Thanks a bunch for the lift. You're a sweetie," she said, closing the door.

A half hour later Carmel came home, poked around in her bag and came up with two one-dollar bills. She wafted them under his nose, then laid them grandly on the table.

"What's this for?"

"Payin' off my debt. On account. I'll come up with another two next week—or the week after for sure."

Jesus, the futility. "You have the rent due this week," he reminded her.

"Just never mind that. I got it saved out o' the household expenses money you give me. Now you be a good boy 'n' take these bills, Jules, hear me?"

"I hears you."

She got out of her coat, lit the oven and sank with an expiring sigh into the brown corduroy-covered armchair they'd found at a Goodwill shop. The two rooms, a wasteland before, were becoming so cluttered one was constantly walking around things: lamps, chairs, his books and job paraphernalia which sometimes cascaded off the suitcases piled under the clothes pole; the round solid-oak table was really too large for the *sitting room*, as Carmel liked to refer to it.

"Zap 707 was runnin' a bit rough today. Knockin' away—bdddtttttt every time I stepped down on the gas."

"There a new tenant in four-E," he said, preoccupied. "Paddy for a change. One of O'Hara's burgeoning stable of hustlers."

"I don't like you sayin' that, Jules."

"A twenty-five-dollar black-haired hooker with a Greco-Roman nose."

"You just cut that out now. You got no proof or anythin'."

"Supposing I told you I had your friend O'Hara's ex-wife for fifteen bucks. Which, taking concomitant expenses into account, *handling* charges if you will, was pretty damn expensive vitamin F."

Slumped in the chair, arms dangling over the sides, feet spread, she watched him warily. "You're makin' it up. I don't believe it."

"That's your prerogative."

"I know when you diggin' into me, Jules. You use them big words 'cause you think I'm just a dumb boot. You're gettin' ornery again and takin' it out on me."

"The truth of the matter is I miss the rolling hills of suburban Connecticut."

She kept watching him, on guard, uneasy.

He went into the kitchen, opened the cupboard above the sink. "Would you care for a drink?" he said, elaborately deferential.

"No. And I don't like you goin' so heavy on that King George stuff."

"You're berating me like a fishwife, Carmel."

"Okay. Just keep on keepin' on."

"A bloody goddam fishwife."

"You can take off if you want, Jules. Nobody holdin' a gun to your head."

"I might do precisely that." He tossed the drink down in one swallow, sans ice. Grandiosely.

"Mm-mmh." Carmel rocked her head slowly from side to side.

"At least Gloria was all woman, baby. She loved to ball and she balled." He was glaring at her, trying to stop.

"I never heard o' no Gloria. One more cruel blow." Now Carmel was nodding her head sagely up and down.

"She *loved* it. I don't understand you. You look so frigging good, as if you're *made* for it—but you're neither fish nor fowl. Fish nor fowl!"

Carmel's chin dimpled; a faintly delighted elfin look came over her face. "Fish nor fowl," she repeated, pleased.

"You're not going to intimidate me!" The senseless fury surged, boiled over. He slammed the glass down on the sideboard. It shattered to pieces, blood instantly welling from the base of his thumb.

"What the—ooeee." She hurried into the kitchen, took his hand gingerly by the wrist. "Now look what you done. Gettin' all in a stew . . ."

Rage running out with his blood, he slipped his arms around her, breathing heavily, holding the gashed thumb straight out. "Sorry."

"It's okay, Jules, you're my baby." Arms around his neck, she began covering his face with those rapid bird-peck kisses.

"Why did your shitbox have to konk out on Union Street, just as I came out that door? We'd have never met."

"That's the truth, Jules." Kiss, kiss, kiss, kiss.

"Please let's go to bed."

"Naw." He felt her body stiffen like a pole.

"Please, for Christ's sake—I'm starving. I don't like to beg."

"Naw . . . After supper."

"Now. I'm asking you, please."

Her face broke in pieces.

"I don't want to do it, but I'll do it."

"Take off all the accouterments."

"Dodo."

"Every stitch. Then put on the blue pajamas."

"You put somethin' on that thumb or you gonna bloody me all up."

In the waning light of day she gave in, silent and immobile, her eyes turned to Van Gogh's "Les Vessenots à Auvers."

"You're using that crap on your hair again," he gasped and moments later sank prostrate beside her, face in the pillow. Drained, boneless.

"Are you all right?" he said, voice muffled.

"Yeah."

"How was it?"

"Okay."

He raised his head and saw her face staring upward, engraved like dark stone on the pillow.

"Why did you do it if you didn't want to? I have respect for you. I wouldn't have forced you."

"I don't want you movin' out."

"Do you want to see a psychiatrist?"

"Huh?" The dark eyes flickered with fright. "What for?"

"Never mind." He sank back onto the pillow.

Silence. The air in the room, oven-heated, felt like a warm bath on his back.

She stirred, her fingers tracing his backbone; moving lightly down and absently patting the buttocks. "Hey, Jules . . ."

"Mm."

"What would your mammy say if she saw you now with a—me?"

"A boot?"

"Yeah."

"First of all I don't have a mammy."

"Oh . . . Then you really are my baby. Do you have a daddy?"

"Yes."

"What would *he* say?"

"Goddam, what goes with you guys, anyway."

"*Uh*-huh."

"What would *your* daddy say?"

"Aw, I guess he wouldn't mind—seein' it's you. He'd say, 'The Caucasians is in heat tonight.' "

Jules grinned into the pillow. "Crazy."

Neither spoke for minutes, immersed in a warm stupefying bath. Tranquillity and warmth. The light was fading quickly now.

"Shut the door, Jules."

His eyes flew open, fear unaccountably fluttering like a dead leaf in his stomach; he came instantly up on both elbows, staring wildly at the closed door. "Where—"

"*Je t'adore*, dummy."

"Good Christ." He sank back on the pillow.

"Don't you look now. I'm gettin' up to put my ac- *cou*terments back on."

He heard her dash across the floor to the bathroom, gathering up clothes on the way, in no time at all emerging in the tight jeans and violet sweater. Straight to the telly. "You made me miss part o' 'Hullabaloo.' "

The music came on, medium-slow, heavily accented, rocking. Arms snapping, eyes stark and riveted to the screen, Carmel's body jerked in graceful spastic movements, ball-bearing pelvis synchronized to the after-beat, rocking with abandon. She'd never make love like that.

He watched admiringly. "You got rhythm in your bones, baby."

Arms pumping like a miler now—crazy pelvis!—feet lifting in mincing pony steps, not even breathing hard.

"Sure, all us boots do."

That night he slept his deepest sleep in weeks, toward morning dreaming he was walking the fogbound streets of London with Christine Dubose, the fifth-grade green-eyed charmer transformed to a hip-swinging Soho tart; but beneath the rouge and mascara, the face still artless, ten years old. They strolled hand in hand down a misting cobblestone street, came to a small inn with a mansard roof and were shown to a room by a silent uni-formed woman carrying a massive brass key ring. Case-ment windows were drawn shut by the woman, a green candle was lit, and when the woman withdrew he word-lessly lifted Christine in his arms, carried her to the wrought-iron bed and had her there, a sweet and active partner gazing all the while into his eyes with a heart-breaking glitter-green sorrowful gaze. "I adore you," she whispered wantonly, "I adore you." He awoke to pale sunlight, feeling weightless, his eyes washed and tears on his cheeks. This one he'd keep to himself; he wouldn't ask Carmel for an interpretation of this one.

The melancholia stayed with him most of the day.

Two mornings later he followed Carmel to the Texaco station, where she left the Dodge with Mario for a check-up. The knocking had been getting worse. He drove her to Mrs. Cameron's and picked her up at five.

They were stopped at a traffic light on Van Ness when she suddenly grabbed his arm. "Jules, lemme dash to that box. I forgot to mail this this mornin'."

"What is it?"

"My new poem."

"Hurry up."

She scurried to the curb in her yellow bandanna, a lissome twenty-year-old Hattie McDaniel. The waste of energy, the futility, he thought. Two days from now the presses would stop at *Mademoiselle* when her manila envelope arrived.

Behind him someone lightly tapped a horn. Glancing up at the rear-view mirror, he saw Mergy smiling faintly, nodding at him. His mouth went dry. Had he seen her get out of the car, or had he just pulled up? Probably the latter. *I don't require a lecture on civil rights, Roman.* Carmel was on her way back; if the light turned to green now he could casually turn the corner, circle the block and pick her up. Treat it as a practical joke. The light stayed red; Carmel opened the door and slid back in.

"There, that's done."

Against his will he shot another glance at the mirror and saw Mergy's face impassive now, eyes straight ahead, slightly dilated. Another fall from grace.

"Jules—the light. People're honkin'."

He went to the gas and the car jumped forward.

"What the devil . . ."

The hell with it. He wouldn't be intimidated.

At the Texaco station Mario told them he'd had time only to give the Dodge a cursory check. He suspected it was the rod bearing, and could they leave it one more day?

"I need it for work. I'll bring her in again over the weekend," Carmel said.

He followed her home, the rapid-fire *bdddttttt bup-bupbupbupbup* like a malfunctioning jackhammer barking in his face whenever she accelerated from a stop.

After supper Carmel turned on the TV and he watched in dismay as she sank to the mattress in her cross-legged Pocahontas position. He told her he was going out for a walk and went upstairs to Henry's pad, hungering for a game. There was no reason why they couldn't get back on a neighborly basis; so long as they stayed away from his car their business was their own affair. He wouldn't entreat, simply ask in a casual off-hand way, "Anything doing tonight?" Approaching the door, he heard voices from within; he knocked, waited. No answer. He was sure the voices had come from Henry's place. He knocked again: no sound at all now.

Stooping to the keyhole, he got a cameo view of Long-well sitting on the divan at the far end of the room, naked to the waist, his taut narrow face turned toward the door, intent, frowning slightly while his brown fingers, as if with an animal life of their own, perfunctorily kneaded one of the bare milk-white breasts of Trudy Lester.

Seventeen

The call came while they were gathered in Mergy's office for the weekly pep talk, this one dealing specifically with the matter of recent ragged results from the predominantly Spanish-Mexican Mission District.

Mrs. Grady, the receptionist, knocked and stuck her head in the door. "Excuse me, phone for Roman."

"Take the message, please," Jules said.

"She said it's an emergency."

He looked at Mergy. He was still on a predominantly "Jules" basis with him but there had been an ever so slight chill in the air of late, a detectable cutting edge to Walter's cordiality.

"We'll wait if you'll make it snappy."

He went into the outer office and picked up the receiver.

"Yes."

"Get ready for a shock, Jules."

"What is it? I'm busy."

"You better set yourself."

"For Jesus' sake, *what?*" he said in a low tense voice.

"It's ZAP 707."

He waited, mute.

"She shit out, Jules. All of a sudden. Just went phhhhht."

He let his breath out slowly in genuine despair. "I can't come now. Where are you?"

"Lessee—Polk and uh—Pacific. How'm I gonna get to work?"

"Take a bus, people do it every day!" he said, his voice rising. "Who are you, the Queen of Sheba?" He saw Mrs. Grady's eyelids flutter.

"I don't think so. What about the jalop?"

"I'll get to it later. Leave it unlocked. I have to hang up."

"Jules . . ."

"*What?*"

"Shut the door."

He banged the receiver down.

Mergy let them go forty-five minutes later. Equipped with a new memorandum on the handling of "cultur-ally-deprived respondents in disadvantaged areas," Jules was just getting in the Plymouth when Mrs. Grady called down the street to him, "Phone. Same party."

He went back in, lifted the receiver and said care-fully, "What's the matter?"

"I guess I'm gonna get in trouble for this."

"You might."

"It's me again."

"Hello, me." He shook his head rapidly from side to side. Mrs. Grady was watching him.

"I had to hear your voice."

It took a really supreme effort to say again, "What's-the-matter?"

"I'm sick o' cleanin'. I'm depressed. Are you still my friend?"

He waited.

"Jules?"

"Yes."

"I broke Mrs. C's second-best vase a while ago."

"What else is new?" Disembodied, he heard his voice, flat, metallic, syllables evenly spaced.

"I know you don't like me callin' there but I had to hear your voice again. Why'd you hang up on me?"

"I'm going to do it again."

"Shut the door, shut the door," she said in singsong and the line clicked dead in his ear.

He spent a rough afternoon in the Mission District— no shacks in the woods, teepees or brush huts, but even more depressing: one downgrade flat after another, pressing the gilt pocket flashes and Better Business Bureau leaflets on uncomprehending stolid-faced suety women—and at a quarter of five called the A A A to pick up the Dodge and tow it to the Texaco station.

He drove in a half hour later.

"It's what I suspected," Mario said, "she's thrown a rod. It would cost more to fix than she's worth."

Another precipitous fall from grace.

"Hundred thirty bucks down the drain," he said glumly.

"You paid that much?"

"Yes. Why?"

"That's high. I would have guessed, considering the general condition, sixty—seventy-five tops."

A one-in-five-hundred bargain with surprisingly sound

tires, Henry had said.

"Fuck Mr. Roman," he murmured.

Mario leaned forward. "Pardon?"

"You couldn't tell if the tires are the same ones that were on when we last brought it in, could you?"

Mario looked at him oddly. "I wouldn't remember that."

Jules abruptly slapped the mottled front fender with his palm. "Would you care to purchase the remains?" Theatrically, like a carnival shill.

"I couldn't offer you more than ten dollars."

"Accepted."

Jules checked the glove compartment for personal belongings and came out with three pencils chewed to the quick and the jar of goo Carmel used on her hair. Haverstock's Hair Food, the label read: Rich in lanolin with Vitamins A D & F.

He signed the certificate of ownership. Mario, handing over the ten, asked casually, "How's your lady friend these days?"

"A royal pain in the ass if you want to know the God's truth."

On the stairway he met Trudy Lester coming down. "Hello there, Buster."

"Miss Lester."

"I thought you'd be using your rain check before now."

His gaze fell briefly to the taut blouse-encased breasts, remembering how white the one had looked cupped in Longwell's hand, then came up again, focusing involuntarily on the bump in her nose. "How about now?"

"Sorry, I'm on my way out. You're terribly serious. Do you ever smile?"

"Only when there's something to smile about."

"Excuse *me*. For asking. Got to run." She lightly tapped his shoulder with a tapered silver nail and edged past him, heels clicking seductively down the wooden stairs.

At the row of mailboxes on the third-floor landing he saw that Carmel's poem had been returned, the envelope folded and jammed into the box. *Mademoiselle* regrets. He wondered if he should go upstairs and tell Henry and Longwell about the Dodge and Mario's evaluation, watch their faces and try to get an inkling of whether they'd actually paid the hundred thirty. Damn. Why hadn't he gone with them? If they *had* paid the entire sum there might be a possibility of getting part of it back. Have the whole barracks, Reba Mae in the vanguard, converge on the used-car dealer. Mass intimidation (integrated). But he'd just sold it! A sawbuck for a ton and a half of metal. Could *Mario* possibly have conned him? Weary of thinking, he poured himself a King George IV and sat in the Goodwill chair staring at "Les Vessenots à Auvers," discovering that if you squinched your eyes in a certain way so as to alter the contours of the vegetation, it really looked a bit like the rolling verdant Connecticut countryside.

Carmel came home at seven with two TV enchilada dinners. "I see King George and you is havin' another little chat. I hope you're in a better mood than—uh-oh." Her gaze fell on the manila envelope. "My poem. They scrunched it all up." Grave-eyed, she tore open the flap and read the rejection slip. "Life keeps on dealin' these blows."

"Maybe the time isn't yet ripe for another Edna St. Vincent Millay."

"Huh?"

"Come here." He reached out, took her hand and drew her down on his lap, hating himself for yielding to the sarcastic impulse. It was so unfair, the girl was a child. And the worst thing you can do, he remembered—"the unkindest cut of all" was the way the pince-nezed supervisor of elementary schools had put it in a pre-term lecture to new teachers—"is to condescend to your charges, compensating for your own inadequacies by indulging in sarcasm which they do not comprehend and against which they have no defense." Agreed. Only he'd never had an opportunity to indulge himself; his charges had always jumped him before he could open his mouth.

"Keep writing," he said. "Keep on keepin' on, Edna."

"You startin' to talk like one of us, Jules." She pecked at his nose and eyes. "You're my baby."

"No, it's the other way around."

"Man, I is beat. I had to change buses twice to do the shoppin' and all. I was gonna call back and ask you to pick me up but you was soundin' kinda hot under the collar this mornin', callin' me the Queen of Sheba an'—"

"Auvers," he said, squinching an eye, "looks rather like Tolland County, Connecticut."

"The jalop!" She sat up straight. "Did you get it?"

"It's totaled out. Worthless. Mario gave me ten bucks for it."

"Ah, what a blow, Jules."

"He said he thought it was worth seventy-five tops before the trouble."

"Is that a fact."

"Scarcely a one-in-five-hundred bargain."

Carmel sat clucking softly, dazedly shaking her head.

"Do you think it within the realm of possibility that your brother and Henry pocketed about fifty bucks of mine?"

"Now, Jules, you stop that. You're so suspicious. Longwell done a couple bad things in his life but he ain't no thief."

"You know Henry switched my tire that night, don't you? There's no question of it."

"Jules, that was months ago and you never had no definite proof at-all. If you did you should've gone to him about it. You thought they was messin' with your jalop last week and you was wrong, wasn't you?"

"They're stealing people blind in that parking lot. There's going to be trouble."

"Well I tol' Longwell, I don't know what you and Henry is up to but you be careful. And he said they ain't up to nothin' and to shut my big boot mouth."

"I'm surprised they haven't approached you regarding a caper at Mrs. Cameron's. Jesus, it would be a piece of cake. Inside job. Loot the silver and brass candlesticks, the family heirlooms."

"She ain't got no brass candlesticks. I wish I knew when you was jokin'." She drew back and studied him with a bright-earnest stare. "You sure are actin' strange these days. Neither fish nor fowl, fish nor fowl."

He grinned in spite of himself, feeling the strain in

his face. "You really are insane. We're attuned."

"I don't know nothin' about that but I got somethin' that'll make you feel better." She scampered off his lap, opened the wicker bag and poked around inside. "Zap 707 may've konked out but I'm stickin' to my debts. Here's two dollars 'n' fifteen—twenty-five cents on account. I'm gonna up the weekly payments, seein' as you'll be pickin' me up and takin' me to work again. . . . Why you shakin' your head like that? You laughin' at me again or what?"

"No, not *at* you . . ." He paused, got hold of himself. "I know something that would make me feel a lot better than your hard-earned money."

"No suh, Jules, you got your vitamin F last week. I'm not slippin' outa no silken ac-*cou*terments for a while yet."

Sometime after midnight, sleepless, trying to track down a maverick among the barrack sounds—the first soft drum of winter rain, he realized presently, at the same time wondering, with a gathering ache in his groin, what it would be like to slip upstairs and knock on Miss Lester's door to redeem his rain check—there came a tentative knocking at their door. His heart banged violently, a wild bird in a cage.

Silence; another knock. Then incredibly the door opened.

"Who is it?" His voice barely made it out of his locked throat.

"It's me, man. Do you have any rubbers?"

Longwell, a thin shadowy wraith inside the doorway.

"What?"

"Condoms, do you have any? I'm up tight."

"No."

Carmel stirred. "Uhhh . . . mmh. Who—"

"Hi, little sister."

"What the—" She came up rigid, staring into the gloom. "Longwell, what you want?"

"Nothing. Go back to sleep. Sorry, man, but it was urgent. Pill problem."

"That's all right."

The door closed softly.

"What'd he want?"

"Rubbers." The banging in his chest slowly subsided.

"Man, you'd think F was more important than A, B, C, D around here."

"What was the lock button doing down?" he said, getting mad now.

"I dunno. I must've left it."

"Damn, that's why I used to bolt it! You see what can happen!"

"It was only Longwell. What you so afraid of?"

"How could he just walk *in* like that!"

"Well, you brought up sleepin' three to a room and it ain't too hard."

"What if we had been *doing* it?"

"Like I said earlier there was no danger of that, Jules." She reached over, gingerly patted his leg.

Incensed, he threw back the covers, stomped across the cold floor and attached the chain fastener. Pulled the door viciously against it a half-dozen times, checking the tensile strength, then jammed up the lock button.

He came back to bed, mute, breathing hard.

"Okay, you satisfied," Carmel sighed. "King George Four himself couldn't get in now."

Eighteen

Carmel was settled in at the window table of Dante's Excelsior Coffeehouse the following Saturday afternoon when the man in the brown suit and gray fedora came to the barracks asking for Longwell.

"He's upstairs. Four-C," Jules said.

"Your nameplate says Brown."

"That's his sister. You'll find him upstairs." With a stab of foreboding Jules studied the man's heavy, impassive face. "What do you want him for?"

"Thank you." The man tipped his hat and turned to the stairway.

Jules stayed in the doorway, uneasy, listening up the stairwell for voices. He thought fleetingly of dashing to the phone, calling up to warn them, but he stayed rooted, listening. Now a door opened above him; there was a murmuring of voices, nothing he could make out. The door closed. Silence. He waited another minute or two, the feeling of dread abating. It was all right. There was no problem, as Elmer would say. Why should there be a problem? He turned to go inside and the upstairs door opened again. Presently the brown-suited man and Longwell came down the stairway abreast, handcuffed together. Longwell's gaze froze him with a look of loathing. He said in a soft even tone, "Thanks a lot, man."

Jules closed his eyes and pressed his head against the door jamb, sick at heart. And a moment later opened his eyes on Henry's maroon turtleneck sweater.

"Why'd you have to go tell the man, Jules?"

"I had no way of knowing. He didn't have a badge—"

"A boy in the prime of his life whisked away like that. Couldn't you figure it out—a white man snoopin' around dressed up for business? Who'd you think it was?"

"Was it the . . . draft or the tire business?" he heard himself say.

Henry's cherubic face seemed to tighten and quiver. "What you mean the tire business?"

Numb, mute, Jules shook his head from side to side.

Reba Mae materialized on the lower landing. "What's Longwell doin' chained to that man? I saw out the kitchen—"

"The draft board came and got him," Henry said.

"He had no badge. I didn't know who he was."

"Huh." Reba Mae gazed heavily up at them.

"I better go find someone about a lawyer," Henry said and hurried down the stairs. Reba Mae remained on the landing, ponderous, her big dark face trembling slightly as with palsy, absently wiping her hands on her apron.

Jules went back inside, ate the rest of the Kona coffee direct from the carton, standing in the open refrigerator door. He found the morning's classified section in the pile of newspapers under the sink and sat down at the table, poring intensely over the Apartments for Rent columns, forcing himself to concentrate. A tight strip of pain squeezed his chest like a wire band. He went to the phone to call the numbers he had circled, dropped the paper and sat in a kind of stupor, racked with guilt, for close to half an hour—finally brought out of it by the sound of high heels on the stairway.

Heart thumping, he crossed to the door and opened it.

"Hello."

"Hi, Smiley."

"How about that rain check?"

"Sure, come on up." The heels clicked deftly past him, smooth bare calf muscles shifting fluidly before his eyes as he followed her up.

Her apartment contained a bright-green rug and small, dark-wood furniture, all new. The divan, cocoa-colored, sat snugly under green drapes.

Jules closed the door after them, clearing his throat. "How much?"

"Same as yours—sixty-five."

"No, I mean . . . how much?"

Taking off her coat, she turned and stared at him. "What are you talking about?"

He gazed back at her in dismay. Another one of those red-letter Fuck Mr. Roman days. He said wanly, "What exactly did you mean by a rain check?"

She crossed to the closet, hung up her coat. "If you recall, my original invitation was for coffee. I have a rule about people in the same building."

A fat tortoise-shell cat waddled in from the kitchen and plumped down beside the coffee table, yellow eyes big as Jupiter moons.

"What about Longwell?"

She closed the closet door, straightening the coat of a gray pin-stripe suit. "Strictly for kicks."

"I've heard about kicks with colored guys."

The wide gray eyes stared at him, more in disbelief than resentment. "You must be insane. Aren't you living with his sister?"

"Twenty dollars," Jules said.

"I said no."

"Forty."

The gray eyes impaled him. "Just this once. I don't want you after me."

"All right."

She kicked off her shoes and walked leisurely into the bathroom. An interminable number of minutes passed before she emerged bare-legged, wrapped in a kimono.

The unbridled action took place on the cocoa-colored divan, bump in the nose forbiddingly up close; yellow-eyed cat watching languidly, patently disinterested for all anyone could tell.

He lay on his stomach panting beside her, shivering as the sweat dried, one leg off the narrow divan.

"God, you came at me like there was no tomorrow. Don't you get enough from the sister?"

"She has problems."

"We all do in one way or another, Buster." Her hand pressed dispassionately into the small of his back as she climbed over him. "*Finis.* I have someone coming to dinner."

He dressed slowly, woodenly, the heart gone out of him. F, he decided, is a non-durable, vastly overrated vitamin. He looked in his wallet. "I have seventeen dollars. I'll have to pay you the rest in a day or two."

She sat across the room, ice-calm, expressionless, hands in the pockets of the light-green kimono. "I'm depending on you."

He put the bills on the coffee table. "Whatever you hear around here in the future I didn't fink on Longwell," he said at the door. "The man was in plain clothes—he never showed a badge," he added and drew the door shut behind him.

Nineteen

"I know it wasn't your fault, Jules, now you got to stop dwellin' on it. Henry got us a lawyer."

"If that guy had knocked on any other door in the barracks the result would have been the same. He just didn't look like a cop. Christ, he could have been selling insurance . . . pots and pans. I had no way of knowing."

" 'Course. I called Julius this mornin' and told him. He didn't know nothin' about the draft—and he didn't say so in so many words but they probably came to him like your man without the badge and he told 'em where Longwell was. On top o' that he got his own *police* problems. He said they been harassin' him too. Somethin' goin' on in them cottages, I guess. I tell you, Jules, the roof's cavin'. One blow right on top of another."

"You can say that again."

"One blow after another, Jules." Carmel heaved a prodigious Reba Mae sigh. "Man, I had me a rough day at Miz C's. That woman work me like a slave."

He dumped fresh ice cubes in and poured the Scotch streaming over them. "I'll tell *you* something, Charcoal, I'll trade jobs any time you say. You name it. Would you care to spend seven hours a day trying to talk suspicious old bags and invalid grandfathers into letting you show them year-old issues of idiot magazines for their invaluable opinions? Would you?"

"Well now, Jules, if it's all that distasteful you oughta get in another line o' work. I got no choice at the moment."

"Just what line do you propose?"

"Mmm . . . well, teachin'. Why'd you quit, anyway?"

"One of my students was turning me on. Christine Dubose by name."

"I wouldn't be too surprised, you so F oriented."

"Perhaps Elmer could use an extra hand on Nob Hill with the brooms."

"I don't like hearin' you talk that way. And stop hittin' on George Four. I'm gonna throw that bottle out."

"You do and I'll kick your black butt from here to the Fillmore."

"You better cut out that jokin'. I'm gettin' more 'n' more depressed."

"Why are you so sure I'm joking?" he said and belched.

"Oh, how crass," Carmel fluted. "How utterly vulgar."

He belched again, willfully. "Turn on the set."

"I'm sick o' watchin', Jules. Let's go out somewhere where there's people. We can drop in some places and maybe I can get me another audition."

"And maybe Streisand will turn sepia overnight. I've had enough people today, thank you."

"Can I borrow the jalop?"

"No."

Carmel heaved another world-weary sigh. "I's really depressed. I wonder if Elmer would lend me his."

He turned on the TV: All-Star Wrestling.

Slumped in the Goodwill chair, Carmel grew pensive, absorbed. "I got a secret, Jules. Promise you won't tell."

He nodded, glassily watching the two gross flabby men stalking, grunting.

"My sister Raven and Longwell used to do it when they were kids."

He glanced at her over his drink. "Do it?"

"Yeah."

"How do you know they did?"

"We was all in the same bedroom."

"Good Jesus. Is Jo-jo his—theirs?"

"Naw, it was when we was real young."

He took a few moments to construct the scene in his mind's eye. For some reason it made him feel better.

"You better not tell."

"Maybe it would be grounds for the army rejecting him."

"I'll bite your face."

"No, I'm serious. Moral turpitude or something. . . . Jesus, and I thought I had a strange family." He glanced up at Van Gogh's Tolland County, Connecticut.

"Jules, how would you feel if Jo-jo came to live with us?"

"You're out of your mind."

"Mmnhh, you're always sayin' that lately. I'm depressed. I'm goin' down and ask Elmer for his crate." She got up and poked around the clothes pole, finally choosing the blue-and-green harlequin-pattern dress and her best coat, the one with the white-fur-trimmed collar. Emerging from the bathroom minutes later in full regalia, she said, "Why d'you keep starin' at that picture?"

"When I was a kid there was a field like that in back of our house. On summer nights I used to sneak out in my pajamas and run around barefoot."

"Why'd you do that?"

"I don't know, it was overgrown. I liked the feel of the grass. Damp, cool."

Carmel buttoned her coat, fluffing the white fur at the collar. "Jules?" Her hand was on the door. "Jules."

"What."

"I don't suppose you wanna marry me, do you?"

He shut his eyes, shaking his head ever so slightly, knowing the pain showed etched in his face. She's so dear. It's out of the question. Behind him, gratefully, he heard the door softly close.

The phone rang and he came awake with a start, eyes glazed, focusing on the wrestlers: Fatso throttling Baldy over the ropes.

Head throbbing, synchronized to the jangling, he crossed the room.

"Hello."

"Hello, is this Jules?" a lilting musical voice said.

"Yes . . ."

"This is Gloria speaking."

He waited, frozen; not sure.

"Hi, it's me," a different voice said. "I wanted to cheer you up."

"You didn't succeed."

"Get ready for a shock now, Jules."

"For Christ's sake . . . What?"

"You got yourself set?"

"Not Elmer's car."

"Yup."

He groaned aloud.

"I'm only kiddin'. I wanted to see if you were still mad at me. Are you?"

"No. Come home. I'm going out of my mind here."

"Jules, listen, I got me another audition. I dropped in this cute l'il bar on Clay, Cloud Nine it's called, and they told me to come in Monday afternoon."

"Crazy."

"Aren't you glad?"

"Yes. Come home."

"Okay. You keep away from George now and I'll be home in a shake. Jules, I got this feelin' in my bones. I'm gonna land the job singin' and I'll quit Miz C's and you can come in nights and sip a drink an' watch me. It'll be the beginnin' of my career, Jules. Everythin's gonna be everythin'—I got me a pre-mo-nition. You wait 'n' see!"

Twenty

Three mornings later he found a note under his windshield wiper:

How about the 23
TL

He simply didn't have it; he had asked her to wait another day or two. When he tried to get an advance at the office he'd been told it was against company policy. "Those darky gals don't come that high, do they?" Mergy had added with an odd little smile, eyes averted, inspecting the morning's mail. The guy was weird, devious; neither fish nor fowl. He'd been generally cool since the traffic-light encounter, reverting sporadically to a "Roman" basis, but then, when least expected, he'd turn genial again, coming on with the banter, a breezy off-color anecdote, the wink, grin, slap on the shoulder. There was little doubt of it, the man was a bigot, and there were times when Jules hungered for a direct accounting. "Your personal life is your own business, Roman, I've said it before" (hand light on the shoulder here). "But when it begins to impinge on your future value to the concern, I suggest, if you find yourself unable to alter your mode of living, that we sever relations. *Comprends?*" He would almost welcome it.

Finis, Buster, as Miss Bump Nose would say.

Longwell had been police-escorted back to Los Angeles and the freeze was on in earnest at the barracks. It
would be a long day's journey before Henry again
wished him a pleasant night's sleep, and Reba Mae and
Elmer were ostensibly sporting blinders when he passed
them on the stairway. He was falling from grace all over
the lot. The shock of a friendly countenance these days
would likely knock him on his ass. (Even Horsback
trotting up at the moment and whinnying "good morning" would be a welcome respite.) Welcome to California. Well, if things got much worse there was one alternative—a craven ace in the hole: recross the wide
Missouri and reapply for his job at Weaver Street. A
grand old school. "Goddam, what goes with you?"
would be Earl's effusive greeting, and H. B. Ellis would
turn apoplectic, stammering inarticulately. *Shocked and
appalled, sir, that you should take it upon yourself . . .*
Exhume the *bête noire.* Out of the question.

That morning, canvassing the Avenues, he had an
eerie experience. The profile of a girl studying a book-
store window display—the fall of dark hair on her
cheek; the way she was standing, weight on one foot,
the other delicately turned out, hands deep in the pockets of a familiar trench coat—sent a wild shudder
through him. Distrait, in a reverie, he went over and
touched her arm.

"Gloria."

She wheeled about, staring with frightened eyes.

"Leave me alone or I'll call a policeman."

"I'm very sorry, I thought—"

"Leave me alone."

He swallowed and walked quickly away, shaking his head rapidly, shaking off the water.

Sic transit gloria. I must be truly going mad.

If he had had the time (and inclination) to make up a list of people who might possibly phone him while watching "The Munsters" that evening—a list in order of decreasing probability—T. Riley O'Hara would have been number fifteen, roughly figuring there were fifteen people in this fabled city with whom he was acquainted.

"Would you come upstairs for a minute. I'm in Trudy's apartment."

"What's it about?" The question, he realized dismally, was rhetorical.

"We'll discuss it up here."

"If it's concerning—" Pocahontas glancing up at him questioningly from the mattress. "All right," he said, and hung up.

"Who's that, Jules?"

"Nothing important. I'll be right down."

Trudy opened the door without a word and he was directly facing O'Hara sitting across the room, arms stretched nonchalantly along the back of the cocoa-colored divan, moldy lumber jacket in a heap beside him.

"I'm here in Trudy's interests," he said pleasantly enough. "The mundane case of the unpaid debt."

"I explained I'd pay as soon as I could."

"What you said was, in a day or two," Trudy said. "That was four days ago. The price was your suggestion." She turned to O'Hara. "He followed me up here like a lost puppy whining for it."

"You're a liar. You came at me on the stairs under false pretenses."

Trudy walked over and planted herself in front of him, close up. "Don't call me a liar."

"Don't call me a whining puppy."

"Will you both—" O'Hara began.

"You were practically on your hands and knees, wagging your tail."

"You're a liar."

Trudy placed her hands on her hips and spat in his face. "Don't call me a liar, you pansy son of a bitch."

"That's a contradiction in terms," Jules said mildly, roiling, feeling his face crimson. He took out a handkerchief and wiped the slime from his cheek. "I suggest you either get your nose bobbed, Miss Lester, or get into some other line of work."

The light-gray eyes flickered murderously; without warning her fingers, hooked claws, came at his face. He grabbed her wrists just in time.

"God damn—hold it!" O'Hara roared. He got up, seized the girl's arm and sent her reeling toward the divan. "It's not worth it—a lousy twenty-three bean!" The coarse filthy reddish beard was almost in Jules' face. "When can you pay?"

"This weekend." His breath was coming quick and shallow, catching in his throat.

"Put the money in an envelope and slip it under the door. If it isn't here by Saturday night, you've had it, Friend."

"How d'you mean, had it?"

"Every which way."

"If you're considering telling Carmel, that's useless. She's unconcerned about the source of my vitamin F."

O'Hara stared, uncomprehending. "You're a bona-fide freak, do you know that?"

Jules felt strangely lightheaded; he almost swayed.

"Fuck you, Van Gogh, you're not intimidating me."

The stone-blue eyes blazed into his. "You must be deranged. Where did you come from? Out of what hole? You ought to go back to wherever you crawled out of, Friend, you're bad news. You've been spreading garbage about me, you finked on the girl's brother—"

"You're a cheap pimp and a fucking liar," Jules stated and smashed his fist into the filthy beard. O'Hara reeled backward, legs lifting awkwardly like a colt rearing, barely managing to keep balance. Wondering what to do next, Jules caught a fleeting glimpse of the cat's moon eyes under the divan; he didn't see the girl come at him but felt five distinct nails raking his cheek, his mind playing the uncanny trick of conjuring five stubs of chalk in the wire music-staff holder; whenever he used it the chalk always screeched on the blackboard, the kids stuck fingers in their ears. He put his hand to his cheek and it came away smeared but discernibly patterned, quintuple crimson streaks.

"Get out of here," O'Hara said. "I warn you, take off fast before something happens."

Jules went calmly to the door and opened it, hand clamped to his face. He felt marvelously loose, resilient, near-exultant. "The money will be here by Saturday evening. And I meant it about your nose," he said in an almost solicitous tone to Trudy. "For Jesus' sake do something about it as soon as possible," he said and pulled the door shut behind him.

Down the steps, springy, two at a time, hand frozen to his cheek.

Carmel, back hunched, chin in palms, looked up as he went past her. "What the devil . . ."

Into the bathroom, soaking a face cloth in cold water; warily he withdrew his hand, watching the mirror. Raked good. Scarred for life. He clamped the dripping cloth to his cheek.

"Now what the devil's happened?" Carmel came in behind him.

"Nothing, nothing at all—except for one little thing. The fucking roof's collapsed."

"What you—lessee." She pulled the hand holding the cloth away, her eyes bugging. "Ooeee. How that happen, Jules?"

"Will you for Christ's sake let go."

"Who done it? The person who called you? . . . Who'd you see upstairs, Jules?"

He closed his eyes, letting the ice water sting the wounds. Nile overflowed its banks good this time. A bona-fide rampage.

"Did you have a fight with Henry?. . . Jules, why aren't you tellin' me?"

"Shut up for a minute, will you?"

"I'm goin' up there."

He heard her go out and gingerly took away the cloth —revolted by his ripped flesh. Soaked the blood out and applied it again. In the other room he got the telephone receiver clamped under his chin and awkwardly dialed Operator with his left hand.

"Person to person to Arthur Roman, Willimouth,

Connecticut, 2–7423."

He waited through five rings, then heard Arthur's voice, sleep-heavy. "Hullo."

"Arthur Roman?"

"Yes."

"San Francisco calling. Go ahead, please."

"Arthur, it's Jules."

"Where have you been? Is anything wrong?"

"Sorry I woke you. I forgot about the time difference."

"Kid, are you all right? Dad's worried. We wrote three or four letters. You never answered."

"I didn't get them. Arthur, listen . . ." He heard his voice quaver, amazed by the sting of tears in his eyes. "Could you possibly use me to help out at the theater? Just temporarily . . ."

There was a dread pause at the other end.

"Jesus, kid, I'm barely keeping my head above water here. Business is really terrible. Haven't you worked at all since you left?"

"I have a job."

"Doing what?"

"Just a job. Arthur, I'm sorry I woke you . . ."

"Wait a minute. Are you at a different address? Why didn't the letters—"

"Arthur, please don't tell Dad about this call."

"Give me your address and this phone number."

"Don't tell Dad. Please. My love to Mary."

He hung up and sank back in the chair, holding tight to the wet cloth dripping unheeded onto his shirt, staring stolidly at Van Gogh's Tolland County.

Carmel came back downstairs.

"Welcome to Connecticut and good luck to you, Carmel."

She stood silently over him, austere, eyes grave.

"Jules, what that white girl tear you up like that for?

Twenty-One

He called in sick the next two days—he couldn't very well go out into the field with a raked cheek, much less show his face at the office (envisioning himself explaining to Mergy that the five stripes had been effected by a weird encounter with a wire music-staff holder)—and steered clear of the barracks denizens by the simple expedient of not stepping foot outside 3-B. He let Carmel take the car to work; he at least owed her that (reparation for conspicuous disloyalty). Somehow it didn't matter any more, what would happen would happen; it was in the laps of the gods. And in a lackadaisical kind of way he rather enjoyed the prospect of tempting fate with the company Plymouth. "Someone gotta go out and bring home the bacon," she'd said that morning, bathing his face. "I'll try to get a advance from Mrs. C. Forty dollars. Mmmh. That mighty expensive vitamin F, Jules." Listless, brooding, he sat between the Van Gogh and the TV and reflected that for most of his short adult life he'd either avoided or lost every major encounter: trampled by the ten-year-old Weaver Street hordes, letting that vicious bitch landlady intimidate him almost to the point of mayhem (and still at it, quite likely throwing out his mail); he'd backed out of the Fillmore excursion to locate Longwell (O'Hara gloating witness to his fear!), balked at confronting Henry with the twin matters of the switched tire and the $130 clinker Dodge. But at least he'd got in one good smash to Van Gogh's beard. Jesus, that had felt good, and the scars on his cheek could be worn like a badge of first valor.

Probably should have married Gloria. That might have been the one memorable mistake. He wouldn't be in this morass today. Should have asserted himself, taken charge, cut down her martini intake—the drunken free-wheeling directionless nights were what had both exhilarated and scared him—laid down the law. *We're getting married, Gloria, this is much too good to lose.* Stopper the gin, dam up the Nile . . . And without raising a finger, passive to the end, he'd let her go to the history instructor, Sandstone or Sundstrom, a pallid lavender-and-lace type with a voice ever so soft and an incongruous Cesar Romero mustache. No more lollipops. The first time they'd made love, jubilant, out of his mind it was so good, he'd withdrawn momentarily, so anxious to prolong it. . . . *Oh don't, that's like taking a lollipop out of the hands of a child.* The next evening, stretched out on the sofa, studying, she'd suddenly banged the textbook shut hard, with authority, turned those hungry green eyes on him. "It's lollipop time, Roman," she said. No more lollipops. Nevermore.

Friday night Carmel came home with twenty-three dollars.

"Mrs. C said she didn't believe in advances but I got it from someone."

"Who?"

"A friend. What you been up to all day?" He saw her eyes furtively check the level in the George Four bottle.

"What friend do you have with that kind of money?" he pressed.

"It was Henry. Jules, you better shave, you're gonna look like Santa Claus."

"Good God. Does he know what it's for?"

"Now I ain't that dumb. 'Course not. Here, take it."

"You got a good heart, Carmel—considering the circumstances of the transaction."

"Well, I owe you the money and I always figure forgive and forget, live 'n' let live. It's how I was brought up."

"Do me a favor. Put it in an envelope and slip it under her door."

"Now you oughta do that yourself, Jules."

"And put this in the envelope." He scribbled a line on a sheet of paper.

" 'I hereby retract what I said about your nose.' " Carmel read aloud. "Mmh." She shook her head, solemn-eyed, lips pressed tight. "That must've been some trans-*action*."

"Yeah."

At the door she turned tentatively. "Jules, I never known any girls firsthand like that. Does she do most o' the work or what?"

Twenty-Two

Still sleepless in the first gray light of Monday dawn, mind whirling with past trials and present anxieties, he felt the shudder go through Carmel like a jolt of current through a frayed wire. Then she was moaning like a banshee.

He turned over and shook her. The eerie cry terminated with a hoarse catch of breath; his arms, rubber tentacles, wrapped for dear life around his neck.

"I can't control 'em!. . ."

"You're choking me, for Christ—"

"Horr'ble . . ."

"Will you just re—"

"I dreamt I died, Jules."

He gently pried the arms loose. "All right, go back to sleep."

"I can't control 'em any more. It was like I was really dead."

He buried his face in the pillow. "Don't tell me about any more dreams. Please."

She lay rigid in the gathering light, breath gradually quieting to a slow uneven pulse, suddenly shattered by the alarm. Her arm swung out like a mechanical lever. Bang. Off.

He waited, tensing, for the sonic boom of igniting

gas, mad torch-bearing dash to the sink; then she was burrowing back into bed. "It's icy, Jules, gettin' on toward winter."

"There's no winter in this godforsaken town," he said into the pillow. "No snow in Chinatown."

"Are you goin' to work today?"

"No."

"I don't like seein' you like this, it's not healthy for my baby. Lessee the face. . . . She's healin' good, Jules, far as I can see through the beard. Just a few scabs here 'n' there. You oughta take a shower though."

"God bless you too, Cora."

"What you mumblin' about . . . goin' on senselessly. Did you have yourself a good sleep? Is your pants dry? Is they? Hmmm?" Her hand scrabbling under the nonexistent pajama bottoms, tentatively testing the buttocks, then withdrawing fast. "Ecchhhh! Naughty!" He submitted, passive, unaroused, to the insane fictional ritual. Now with a rending bone-weary sigh she sank back on the pillow. "I dunno, Jules, sometimes there's no rest, a body gets weary . . ." She trailed off. He could smell the stale oven heat like vapor off hot slate pouring into the room. You never got that smell from a crackling fireplace in Eastern December.

"My audition's today, Jules, three P.M. I'll have to ask Mrs. C for an hour off. She ain't gonna like it."

Christmas in Connecticut, he thought. Snowlight in Vermont.

"You gonna let me take the car again?"

"Be my guest."

"I'm bein' awful careful, Jules. *Je t'adore.*" She was on top of him, nibbling at his ears. "I gotta get up an' face the day, bring home the bacon for my baby." Sighing enervated fat-woman sighs, she eased out of bed, padded to the bathroom. He lay quiet and boneless, listening to the muffled sounds, toilet flushing, tin-drumming water; then the kitchen-clatter of pots and dishes, heavy clunk of an empty bottle dropped in the garbage pail. "Shitty ol' George Four," he heard her murmur.

She paused at the door. "You sure you don't wanna come to the audition with me?"

"I'll forgo that pleasure, thanks."

"Huh? You always mumblin' into that pillow. I don't like seein' you this way, Jules. Promise me you'll go outside today. If you don't I'll get depressed."

He nodded into the pillow, gratefully heard the door being unlatched, opened, softly drawn shut.

He dozed off and woke up around ten, sweltering. Raised himself with a groan and shut off the oven; shuffling into the bathroom to inspect his cheek. Better. He should shave, call the office, tell them he'd be in tomorrow barring complications. . . . Much better, thanks. . . . Yes, the fever's down. . . . Mm-hmm, seems to be quite a lot of it goin' around. . . . Some chicken broth would be fine, preferably the Southern frahd variety if it ain't too much trouble. You're a jewel, Miz Cameron. . . . Excuse me—Mr. Mergy. And my very best to Jean. And to Gloria Mundi: in memoriam. Nevermore.

He spent the morning naked playing five-card stud with an alter ego, steadily upping the ante and quitting when he had amassed forty dollars (the going price of vitamin F) by the expedient of taking over the opposing hand when the deal was more propitious to that side.

Toward noon he turned on the tube, watched a few minutes of "Guiding Light" and shut it off, almost twisting the dial off the casing. Back into the bathroom like a sleepwalker, running the shower flood-tide and steam-hot, wallowing in the Nile. He stood in it until his skin wrinkled.

Dressed in comfortable accouterments, minus four days' growth of beard, he cautiously stuck his head out the door, reconnoitering: coast clear. He hurried down the stairs into mild December sunlight, blinking, and walked somnambulant toward Powell Street, a walk in the sun, craving the proximity of the elegant Nob Hill towers. Some area with an iota of class for sweet Jesus' sake . . .

He found himself a half hour later in the men's room of the Fairmont Hotel, brought there by a call to nature and a yearning for compassion. Business was fairly brisk in the aseptic beige-tiled chamber. He relieved himself at the urinal and was zipping up when Elmer lumbered toward him in a starched white jacket, an uncustomary smile frozen on the broad flat face, whisk broom at the ready.

With recognition the smile melted like frost in the sun, leaving barren brown earth; broom poised in mid-air.

"I won't require your services, Elmer, this coat really doesn't warrant it. How are you?"

Elmer nodded glumly, his gaze fixed on Jules' right cheek.

"The result of an altercation in Miss Lester's apartment. You might have heard about it."

"Heard somethin' about a scuffle."

"I've never been in your place of business before. It's really quite pleasant, immaculate," he ran on, glancing about him self-consciously, "a lot more cheerful than mine, I can assure you . . ." and was brought to his senses by Elmer's growing scowl. "Listen, you don't believe I finked on Longwell, do you?"

"I don't know nothin' about it."

"The man who came to the door was in plain clothes. No badge. I had no way—I wouldn't do that to anyone, friend or enemy. Do you believe me?"

"You're awright, Jules, but you don't belong there. You'd do better stayin' with your own folks."

Jules seized on the glimmer of compassion as at a straw. "Outside of Carmel you're my only friend there, Elmer. Do you know that?"

Elmer shifted uneasily, eyes averting to an influx of gentlemen through the leather-padded door. "I'm going to be busy now."

"Why don't I belong there? For Christ's sake aren't we all born equal?" he blurted, at once meaning it and not for a second believing it.

"I'm not born equal. I wasn't born to stand in no toilet." Elmer turned away, synchronizing the first flick of his broom to the termination of a white-haired gentleman's zipping-up process.

You might be out of place in the rolling hills of Tolland County, Elmer, he thought, but you'll never slit my throat. "I'll take home some of these matches if I may."

"Help yourself," Elmer said, whisking away while urinals gurgled and the white-haired gentleman, grim-faced, fumbled in his pocket.

At the barracks he put his hand on the phone to be-latedly call the office and it went off in his face; his heart shot up to his mouth.

"It's me. Set yourself."

"Don't screw around, will you?"

"I'm not, Jules. Get yourself set for a shock."

"The car," he said evenly, going along, still not be-lieving her; he'd never really been able to tell.

"Yep."

"I'm not in the mood for screwing around," he said weakly.

"Naw, it's for real, Jules. Life's dealt us a bad one this time. Promise you'll still be my friend."

Now he believed her and slumped against the wall, closing his eyes. *Mrs. Gloria Sundstrom, please, Department of History, U. of Conn. Storrs.* "How bad?"

"You better come, Jules. There's people gatherin' around and a cop. The whole schmeer."

"Where?" he asked, almost lackadaisical now; he hadn't really believed fate would go for the bait.

"Jackson and—wait, lemme take a peek out—Hyde."

"Can the car be driven?" he said, his mind's eye re-verting to Mergy. No mere fall from grace this time, not by a fucking long shot; more like a headlong plunge off the Bay Bridge.

"Jules, you better come on . . ."

Twenty-Three

In a mild stupor he stared at the cab driver's profile for minutes before it registered. He leaned forward.

"Do you by any chance recall picking me and a young lady up in front of the King of Hearts a couple of weeks ago?"

The driver craned around momentarily. "I never saw you before."

"I left my sport coat in the back seat of this cab."

"If you did, another fare got it."

"Are you about a size forty?" Jules heard himself say.

The driver shot a brief glance at the rear-view mirror, then veered to the curb and braked sharply.

"Okay, Jack, out. No charge."

"It's possible I'm mis—"

"I've had enough bullshit for one day. Out." The driver leaned across the seat and pushed the door open.

He watched the cab slew angrily away on the cable-car tracks. Well, I'm really cracking up. I don't believe any of this. He waited in a daze until another cab spotted him from the wrong side of the street, shot past him, executed a U at the intersection and came barreling back as if to run him down. He gave the address and kept his mouth shut until they arrived at the corner of Jackson and Hyde.

Disembarking, he saw that the front end of the Plymouth was stove in. The right front wheel and fender of the other car were crumpled, both vehicles forming a perfect V in the middle of the intersection. An exemplary job of bringing home the bacon. Carmel was standing angularly, stiff as sculpture, beside a plumpish woman in a print dress who was talking with vehement gestures to a young cop. The cop, head seemingly bent under the tirade, was writing on a pad.

Thirty or forty bystanders watched Jules get out of the cab and approach the trio.

Carmel gazed at him with stricken eyes, the harlequin-pattern dress garish in the bright afternoon sun. "Here he is—the man whose car it is, Officer."

"This your car?"

"It's a company car," Jules said, surprised at the evenness of his voice.

"And the young lady?"

"A friend."

"It's what you can expect," the plump woman said stringently.

"Let's have a look at your license and registration," the cop said.

Easy, go through the motions, it will be over with shortly; no worse than waiting out a nightmare. He brought out the papers, feeling disembodied. From the circumstances of the collision it had evidently been Carmel's fault. The woman regarded him with stony disdain as they exchanged information. She said in a low flat voice, "You ought to know better than to let those people drive your car."

Calm and composed, don't let them break your back.

"We're all born equal, lady."

"My husband is an attorney. He'll see that the insurance people receive all pertinent information."

"Crazy."

He got in the Plymouth and tried to start the motor. It whirred hopelessly a few times, then to his mild astonishment turned over and caught; an accompanying *k-cunk, k-cunk, k-cunk* sounded from the innards. Carmel got in beside him, slumping way down in the seat. "Life just keeps on dealin' 'em."

The cop came over to Jules' window. "Your radiator's leaking, buddy."

"Thank you."

"And *I* have to call a tow truck," the plump woman fumed.

Jules eased the car back with an excruciating drawn-out wrenching sound as it disengaged from the opposing fender. He saw the plump woman gasp, then squeeze her mouth and eyes shut, looking for a fanciful moment like an outsized Pekinese. Now he eased forward, the blur of white curious faces making way, gazing stolidly in on them.

They drove a half-dozen blocks in silence, the *k-cunk, k-cunk, k-cunk* of fan blades against radiator reverberating like gunshots down the sunlit street. He looked back once, noting the spoor of water behind them.

"Are you still my friend?"

His breath came out in a languid helpless sound of mirth.

"God bless, Jules, you're laughin'."

"Don't be fooled. I'm crying on the inside."

"You see how things happen to me. One/ another."

"It's more like you happening to them."

"Yeah. I guess I'm just a bonehead."

"You really brought home the bacon this time, Charcoal. In spades. Excuse the expression."

"Ah, Jules, don't get mad at me. I'm depressed enough."

"I had a fairly decent day until this. I visited Elmer, I walked on Nob Hill with my face in the sun."

"Yeah, I can see you got yourself a little color. And you shaved the whiskers. . . . Now why you laughin'? I don't like you doin' that. There you go shakin' the head again, just shakin' away. . . ."

With an effort he came out of it. "Do you still want to go to the audition?"

"No, I can't hack it. I got the shakes too, Jules." She hugged herself. "An' I told Mrs. C I'd be back at four. I can't hack that either."

"You had a feeling about the audition. Everything was gonna be everything. You practically guaranteed it."

"Yeah, I know. But I couldn't o' foreseen this blow. Fat-ass paddy came outa nowhere."

"They always come at you out of the blue, don't they?" Slowing for a light, he rested his head briefly on the steering wheel. "If only you hadn't conked out on that block of Union. One block farther on or back and this car would be intact today. My face would be unmarked, Longwell would be sleeping safely upstairs. I might conceivably have a future as field instructor for

Andrew Sylvester. I'd be coming in out of the cold, Carmel."

"You gotta stop dwellin' on those things, Jules. It's not healthy for my baby." She slid over on the seat and dropped a maternal arm around his shoulders. "You gotta keep on keepin' on."

K-cunk, k-cunk, k-cunk. Fan blades driving rivets into his skull, addling his brains.

He pulled into the barracks parking lot, sat in a lethargy as she got out.

"Ain't you comin' up?"

"Is there any cream left?"

"Yeah, Jules," Carmel said, almost smiling.

In the apartment she said, "I guess I gotta call Mrs. C with a story."

"Do me a favor, will you? Tell her the truth for once. Say you were in an automobile accident."

"She ain't gonna believe it."

"Try," Jules said wearily. He went to the refrigerator, dug a few spoonfuls from the carton, then lay down on the mattress, hands behind his head, half listening while she made the call, wondering what fabrication he could pull out of the hat for himself when he told Mergy about the car—*My husband will see that the insurance people receive all pertinent information.* Fatassed arrogant white bitch. Irene, Mrs. Williams, they were all kin. . . . *The roof is truly caving in and I don't seem to have the strength to get out from under. Indeed, sir, an inauspicious beginning in the Golden Gate.* "Goddam, what goes with you guys," he murmured and became aware that Carmel was gazing down on him with that scattered life-done-dealt-another-blow look. The phone was back in the cradle.

"I tol' you she wouldn't believe it, shithead!"

"What?. . ."

"She said my hours was too e-*regular* and not to bother comin' back!"

"Great," Jules sighed, closing his eyes.

"What's *great* about it?"

"I was being ironic," he said gently.

"Huh?" The bewildered brown eyes blazed at him.

"I didn't mean it was great you lost your job for Christ's sake, I—"

"You're always makin' fun of me!"

"I've never made fun of you deliberately."

"You're ashamed of me. And scared. Scared to been seen with me, just sittin' aroun' with your septic nose, scarfin', never goin' out an' boltin' the door cause you're so fearful somebody—"

"Will you for Jesus' sake shut up! I'm not fearful!" Coming upright, feeling the blood in his face.

"Then why don't you take me any place? You think people'll—"

"Why should I? Christ, you're sexless. A frigid boot in a harlequin dress. Why should I risk getting my throat slit? To get laid around here I get hit for forty goddam bucks and a gouged face in the bargain. And you wonder why I don't take you out! That's it in black and white, baby—pardon the expression!" He sank back on the mattress, heart hammering, averting his eyes from the doleful brown gaze.

"Okay, Jules, you don't have to hang around if you don't want. I guess I'm bad news. You take off if you want."

"Never mind. I only half mean what I say."

"Then why d'you say it?"

He shook his head wordlessly.

"I already tol' you why I don't like doin' it."

He flung an arm across his eyes. "Then you ought to see a psychiatrist before it gets worse."

"Now how can I see a psy-*chia*trist, I don't even have no job. You're gonna have to start bringin' home the bacon again."

"I don't know how much longer I can bring it home."

"What you mean by that?"

"Forget it."

"Now I'm really gettin' depressed."

"There may not be any bacon to bring. If I can accurately foresee the official reaction at Andrew Sylvester when they get a look at the crate." He went to the cabinet under the sink, took out the two largest pots and filled them with water. Down the stairs carefully, damn pots too full, water sloshing over; the Nile once again overflowing its banks.

Awkwardly feeding water into the smashed radiator, he glanced intuitively up. Framed in the kitchen window, partly veiled by the curtains, she was gazing somberly down on him—grave, mysterioso: Judith Anderson in *Rebecca*.

"You seem to be having a run of bad luck," Mario said, studying the front end. "She's mashed in pretty good."

"How good—I mean how much would you say?"

"Oh, maybe two hundred—two-fifty. I can bend the fan blades back a bit and put some sealing compound in the radiator. That should last you a couple days or till you get to a garage."

"Crazy."

When Mario finished he looked at Jules not quite directly, lightly licking his lips. "You still seeing the young lady?"

"Once too often," Jules said.

At the bottom of the stairs he heard the commotion, dropped the pots and raced up, through the open door. The kitchen curtains were blazing. Henry was beating at the flames with a broom while Carmel tossed water from a coffee pot in the general direction of the blaze; most of it landed on Henry's head. "Get outa my way, woman!" he roared.

Carmel turned to Jules with terrified eyes. "You dumb dodo—you took all the pots!" she screamed.

Jules seized a blanket off the mattress and began flailing away. The flames leaped, scrabbling up the cardboard walls like something live, disgorging thick acrid smoke.

"It's no use, man—retreat!" Henry yelled, his eyes all whites, round face shimmering with sweat. He turned and dashed out the door, up the stairway, calling in a crazy, high-pitched cracking voice, "Fire! Call the teams! Everyone out! Retreat!"

"Jules, my album! We gotta save—TV!" Carmel wrapped her arms around the monster, trying to lift it off its stand. He grabbed her wrist and yanked her toward the door. The blaze was really crackling good now, eating along the side walls, belching smoke. "The vessels, Jules!"

Pulling her with him, he yanked Van Gogh off the wall, losing a few trees and a cottage in the process, and made it back to the doorway, wheezing, eyes tearing. Others came jostling down the stairway ahead and behind them carrying coats, radios, blankets, Trudy in her green silk kimono, one white breast flopping out—Jules craning around, his gaze insanely riveted on this oasis in a horde of glistening black faces most of which he'd never seen before. "My album, Jules! My mammy gave it—" In front of him there was a crash. Reba Mae stumbling over the pots on the bottom landing and going down heavy. Jules dropped the Van Gogh, got his arms around Reba's massive girth and heaved her up with a strength he couldn't have mustered under normal circumstances. He dragged her with him, one of her feet stuck in a pot, childlike burbling sounds coming from her throat. They lumbered against the wall, ricocheted heavily, then, pushed savagely from behind, lurched out into the parking lot. Something bounded off Reba Mae, scampering between Jules' legs: Trudy's moon-eyed cat.

"The damn pots!" Carmel screamed, and somewhere behind them Henry's voice calling crazily over the din, "The teams—someone call the teams!"

A goodly crowd of nonresident spectators had already gathered in the lot. They watched with alert avid expressions the flames and smoke belching from the kitchen window, other isolated flames now bursting through fissures in the building, and from a corner of the roof, suddenly springing to life like a newborn flower, a shapely spurt of vermilion. Detached from the main conflagration, it bloomed and steadied, quietly blazing like a testimonial beacon of light.

"It was a accident," Carmel whimpered beside him, clutching the tattered Van Gogh, her face still jumping with terror.

"I suppose you were trying to light the oven."

"Naw, Jules—don't tell no one, please . . ."

A few feet away Reba Mae was plumped on the ground, Henry on his knees before her, trying to ease the pot from her foot.

"What happen?" Reba Mae said dazedly.

A siren sounded in the distance, wailing faintly down Pacific.

"Coast o' Maine," Henry mumbled, "got hit by a hurricane."

The siren abruptly soared in pitch and seconds later came screaming into the lot. The huge red hook-and-ladder disgorged a small band of rubber-coated men who began scrambling around furiously, each with a task, wondrously coordinated. But the whole white wooden façade now was a swirling mass of flame, a monumental pyre.

"My album's in there, Jules," Carmel said shakily.

"Better it than you."

"If you hadn't taken the pots!. . ."

"Pots wouldn't have helped, baby, nothing would have. You're too tempting a loser and fate took the bait."

"I ain't no loser!"

Watching the flames licking the barracks clean, seemingly fueled by the pitiful streams of water, Jules felt eerily cleansed, serene. He put his arm around her shoulder. "Nothing to be ashamed of. We're alike—both hung up. Even if you were white instead of black you'd be a loser," he added gently.

"Ah'm not black—I'm brown!" The tears were washing down her narrow face, the grave eyes lifted to his, pool-deep, streaming.

"Right. *Miss* Brown." And if I were king, dilly dilly, then you'd be queen.

"You're white and you ain't drivin' no Rolls-Royce!"

"That's a fact." His arm tightened around her.

Two more teams plunged into the lot, sirens dying while the barracks burned. A few minutes later Elmer came up beside them.

"Saw it from the hill and had a *pre*monition."

Elmer watched the holocaust expressionlessly, with a languorous air of unconcern, like a jaded spectator at a dull parade. So that's what they mean by a state of shock, Jules thought. Hundreds of North Beach residents were filling the lot now, entranced, eyes incarnadine with reflected light, ears tuned to the lively crackling. Some twenty yards away he saw Trudy leaning almost indolently against a car fender, clutching the green kimono tight at her throat, the cat rubbing up against her bare leg.

"Don't suppose there's any insurance," Elmer said after a while.

"I wouldn't think so."

"How'd it happen?"

"Hard to say."

"Wife got a sprained foot." Elmer gazed torpidly at

the picture Carmel was still clutching. "That all you saved?"

Jules nodded. "A dollar-and-a-half print. The world-famous Tolland County, Connecticut."

He dropped her at O'Hara's by arrangement when it was over—there was nothing to salvage—promising to be in touch.

"You can find me here or at Dante's till I figure out what to do. What're you gonna do, Jules?"

"Think. I'll see you in a day or two."

"You better." She gave a little shudder and got out of the car, holding tight to the Van Gogh. "Man, I'm gonna have me some dreams tonight."

Mind clear and blank, he drove aimlessly for an hour or two in the battered Plymouth—knowing it would be his last ride in this particular jalopy—and when it got dark he headed back to the barracks and parked, gazing wonderingly at the charred hull. The frame was still intact, blackened walls visible through glassless windows, cold clean moon light poking into a burned-out honeycomb. Nothing to bolt the door against now, cream all melted in the refrige; George Four consumed, unwittingly fueling the flames. Nevermore.

Toward midnight, pleasantly lost in the immense dark of Golden Gate Park, he pulled to the side of a narrow winding road, took off his shoes and socks and raced mindlessly across a vast stretch of cool grass turned to snowlight by the moon. Gasping, he slowed to a walk, thinking, I own nothing but the clothes on my back and the feel of the grass under my feet. The exquisite chill coursed up his legs and unlocked his mind, sending it ranging across the Missouri to dwell dispassionately but sweetly on God's little acre in Tolland County, then back by the speed of light to an unexpected and uncanny contemplation of the requirements for a California teaching credential and the vague prospect, perhaps unrealizable, of imbuing himself with a newfound steely-willed discipline.

Some time later he drove back to town, the fan blades beginning to clatter again, and checked into the YMCA.

Twenty-Four

The next morning at Andrew Sylvester Research Mergy came outside to look at the car, having listened to Jules' twin unadorned accounts of the Jackson–Hyde collision and Havila conflagration in a state of suspended belief.

The Plymouth sat solidly at the curb, battered but unbowed.

"I'll be a son of a bitch. You've really got problems, haven't you?"

"With the exception of a few magazines the materials are all in the glove compartment. I'd like to take this opportunity to tender my official resignation."

"Gratefully accepted."

"I don't think I'm built for this line of work."

"I couldn't agree more heartily," Mergy said, turning back to the office.

"I have about a half week's pay coming."

"See Mrs. Grady," Mergy said over his shoulder.

"Plenty miles in the old gal yet," Jules murmured, giving the crumpled hood an affectionate farewell pat.

With thirty-seven dollars and forty cents in his pocket he boarded a bus for North Beach, hoping another confrontation with O'Hara would not be necessary to locate Carmel.

She was settled in at the window table of Dante's, clear-eyed, scribbling away as of yore. The harlequin dress looked as though it had been slept in.

"Hey, Jules. . . . How's my baby?"

"You seem none the worse for wear."

"I didn't have too good a night. Reba Mae got O'Hara's bed and I had t' sleep on the floor."

"Like old times," he said, sitting down.

"It's hard facin' the others, Jules. They look at me and don't say nothin', but they know."

"The place was a fire trap. It would have gone up sooner or later. They'll forget."

"Look what O'Hara got me this mornin'," she said, brightening. The new autograph album was bound in soft white leather affixed with a shiny gold lock mechanism.

"I'm not sure you ought to count on an income from poetry right away. What are you going to do?"

"O'Hara said he thinks he can line up some work for me."

"You're not serious . . ."

"What's the matter with that?"

"Jesus, he's really picking the wrong horse this time. Don't you know what kind of work he has in mind?"

Carmel watched him, wary.

"He'll put you out in the streets hustling—talk about crimes against nature! Take it from an old friend, you're better off back in St. Helena."

"Well, now, that was my other thought. I was thinkin' about Jo-jo growin' up durin' these early years. I didn't let on too much when I came back the last time, Jules, but it was kind of a bad scene around the cottages. There was some unsavory-lookin' people about and I think Julius and Margarita are messin' around a little themselves. It just ain't healthy for Jo-jo."

"It's your sister's kid. Can't she—"

"Raven's gone. She took off for Seattle. We're spread all over now 'cept for my old mammy in the grave. . . . Oh, Henry heard through his lawyer friend. The judge is suspendin' execution on Longwell . . ."

"Execution! I hope you mean execution of sentence."

"Yeah, that's it. They're puttin' him in the army."

She was staring unwittingly at his nose; he ran a finger self-consciously along the deviated septic. "He got off easy. I'm glad for him—and relieved."

"What'd that Mr. Sylvester say about the car, Jules?"

"Mergy. Called himself a son of a bitch and gratefully accepted my resignation."

"Uh-oh."

"Best thing that could have happened."

"I just remembered—I left a jar of my Haverstock's Hair Food in the compartment."

"And your heart in San Francisco."

"Yeah." Carmel grinned. "You still crack me up, Jules. When you think of all we been through together. And I ain't forgettin' the hundred two dollars and some cents I owe you on the jalop. I'm keepin' track of it."

"Forget it. Buy yourself another one. With sound tires. . . . Look, it's almost noon. Have you had anything to eat?"

"Naw."

"Are you hungry?"

"I's starved." She popped the album shut, smartly

snapping the gold lock.

They walked down the block to a small Chinese restaurant. Carmel pored over the Oriental entrees, frowning, chewing a corner of her lip.

He gently took the menu out of her hands. "I'll order for you. You'll have the southern-fried chicken and watermelon slice."

"Yassuh," she said, patting his thigh.

It was dark and cool in the small room, blinds drawn; almost nighttime dark, moonless, with a faint incense fragrance.

"You'll come visit me in St. Helena, won't you, Jules? If one of the cottages is empty we can sleep together like old times. You won't need to bolt the door up there."

"Crazy."

Carmel propped her elbows on the table and sunk her chin in her hands, regarding him leisurely, with gravity and love.

"It's kinda sad when you think about it, Jules."

"What is?"

"There's no place left to bring home the bacon to."

Twenty-Five

In the personnel office of the San Francisco Unified School District Building Jules explained his situation, adding, "Please excuse my attire. I was burned out of house and home yesterday."

"I'm sorry to hear that," the woman in charge said. "Do you have your Connecticut credential?"

"Also consumed by fire, I'm afraid."

"We can't do anything for you without the credential. I suggest you send for a duplicate copy immediately along with verification of your teaching experience and a transcript of your college record. As there will be a shortage of teachers for the spring term we can issue you a provisional credential on receipt of your papers."

"Fine."

"You can apply for daily substitute teaching until the spring term commences. For a permanent credential you'll need to complete any course requirements not covered by your Connecticut credential."

"I see."

"I must tell you in advance that virtually all of the spring openings will be in depressed areas."

"Depressed . . ."

"Culturally deprived."

"I've had considerable experience in depressed areas,

though not of an educational nature."

"I always explain this to out-of-state people. Some come from the South and there is an understandable—I say understandable rather than justifiable—reluctance to work with Negro children."

"I understand."

"The most sought-after districts of course—by teachers familiar with our ethnic climate—are in the Oriental sectors."

"Oriental . . ."

"It has to do with the fabric of the family. Disciplinary problems amongst these children are minimal."

"I see."

"Then I assume you would have no objection to teaching in a predominantly Negro district." The woman waited, eyes partially obscured by the glint of fluorescent light from her glasses, lightly tapping a pencil on the desk blotter.

Jules gave it some heavy rapid thought, his short adult life streaming past his mind's eye—but not the vision of a drowning man. It was all a struggle: Elmer in his toilet, Henry scrounging for tires on chill moon-drenched nights; Longwell hauled to boot camp (ass dragging, kicking all the way). And Carmel; but Carmel was something else. Dream merchant, soul sister.

"Keep on keepin' on."

"I beg your pardon?" the woman said, staring.

"Well, if there's an opening in an Oriental district, fine. If not, it really doesn't matter that much."

Don Asher

Don Asher, born and raised in Worcester, Massachusetts, studied at Cornell University, where he received a master's degree in organic chemistry. After working briefly as a schoolteacher and professional musician, he moved to San Francisco in 1959, where he writes and plays the piano in hotels and night clubs. In recent years he has been house pianist at the hungry i and accompanist for The Committee, a satirical revue based in San Francisco. Mr. Asher's first novel, *The Piano Sport*, was published in 1966.